# UNDER GREY CLOUDS

## KAYLIE KAY

ISBN:

ISBN-13: 9781731497161

DEDICATION
*For Lewis xxx.*

# Contents

# Chapter 1

'Bye, Mum,' Lewis shouted above the shrill tones of the school bell that rung out in the playground.

'See you in two sleeps!' Susan called after him, watching proudly as her handsome eight-year-old ran off towards the door, so smart in his private-school uniform of blazer and short trousers, cap perched on his head. She looked around for Sophia, catching a glimpse of her daughter going through the door to the Year 6 block, deep in conversation with her group of girlfriends and clearly even less bothered than her brother that her mum was going away. Susan sighed, but she was grateful it was like this really, it would be much harder if they got upset, and besides, it was all that they had ever known. Mum had always gone away for a few days here and there, but she always came back.

Susan Kennedy could feel the stares and sideways glances of the other mums, all in their sensible mum clothes, a stark contrast to her smart flight attendant's uniform. She knew what they were thinking. How could she possibly leave her children for days? How could she go to work and *serve* people? Well screw them, she thought, they were just jealous really, jealous that they too couldn't get away from the mundanity of motherhood and wifedom, from the school run and the grocery shopping, from looking after their fat, boring husbands. Tonight, she didn't have to think about what was for dinner, whether the kids had done their homework, or whether she needed to receive her husband's advances. Tonight, she would be thousands of miles away, being Susan Harrison.

Susan had never changed her name at work, despite being married to Jeff now for twelve years, because at work she was still her old self, for a few days a month she got to be *her*, not someone's wife or mother. She turned on her stilettos and walked confidently through the school gates to the car park. Still they watched her, as they stood in their cliques, but she couldn't have cared less as she climbed into her brand new Range Rover that was gleaming so much brighter than theirs in the September sunshine.

The motorway was a bitch this morning, she thought to herself an hour later, glad that she had left extra time to get to Heathrow as she crawled along. The phone rang over the Bluetooth and Jeff's name popped up on the screen. She hesitated for a moment before answering, switching herself back from Susan Harrison to Jeff's wife, Susan Kennedy.

'Hi, darling,' she said cheerily.

'Oh, glad I caught you, I thought you may have been at work by now.' Her husband sounded a little flustered.

'No, no, traffic is terrible, I'm still on the M25, is everything okay?'

'Yes, yes, I just bumped into Andy at the office earlier. I've invited him and Evelyn over for dinner at the weekend, I just wanted to check with you, is that okay?' Susan took a deep breath, glad that her husband couldn't see the tortured look on her face, that she only had to fake her voice on this occasion.

'Absolutely, I'd love to see them, I'll make us all a lovely dinner. That's something to look forward to when I get home.' Her happy voice didn't mirror her true feelings.

'Oh, thank you, sweetheart, you really are the best, I do love you.'

'I love you too, Jeff.'

'Okay, well I'll see you when you get back.'

'Bye, darling, try not to miss me too much.'

'You know I always miss you, I wish you'd give up that job.'

'Jeff,' she said in a tone that warned him off going any further.

'I know, sorry, selfish me.'

'Yes,' she scolded kindly. 'You know I love my job. And I love you. Anyway, gotta go, I'm just coming off at the airport now, see you in a couple of days.'

Susan hung up the call and groaned. An evening with Jeff's boring friends was like pulling teeth; she had absolutely nothing in common with them, but she would do it for him, because that was her duty as Jeff's wife.

When she had promised to love him and honour him at the altar she had meant it, and in return he gave her everything she could have ever wanted. She had known that people had judged them because of the age difference, but she hadn't cared, when she was twenty-three he had only been forty-three. He was handsome, and fit, and very, very rich.

Now though, at fifty-five, he was starting to look old, his hair was greying and the pounds had begun to stack on around his middle; lately she had felt the age gap much more. But, she reminded herself daily, while he may not have been fit anymore, and maybe he wasn't quite so handsome, she knew that he loved her absolutely, and he was still very, very rich.

In contrast, she had got more polished, worked out harder, and honed her body to perfection. She looked nowhere near her thirty-five years; at least that's what people told her, and she believed them. No wonder Jeff loved her so much, she looked the part and she was the perfect wife and mother too, and as long as she got her little breaks she could keep it up quite happily.

# Chapter 2

The plane picked up speed as it rolled down the runway, Susan sat on her hands and pushed her head back into the headrest, braced for take-off. There it was, she felt that moment as the huge bird took flight, the air lifting its wings and picking it, and everyone in it, up off the ground. She looked at her watch; 11.55. With a seven-hour-thirty flight time and a five-hour time difference, plus two hours for the airport and bus journey, that would have her in her hotel room for 4.30, she concluded. Perfect.

The ping of the seatbelt signs being turned off signalled the start of work, and Susan got up slowly, stowing her harness into her jumpseat and busying herself setting up the galley ready for the service in first class.

'Excuse me.' Susan hadn't heard anyone come into the galley over the sound of the ovens and the engines. 'Can I get some help with my television please?' She turned around to see a glamorous lady of perhaps sixty years old standing there, looking apologetic.

'Of course, madam, where are you sitting?'

'1G, I'm sorry to bother you.'

'It's no bother.' Susan followed her to her seat and started to help her select a movie. She knew that the older passengers did tend to struggle with the technology, whilst the kids could get to grips with it without any problems. As she navigated the screen with the controller she couldn't help but notice the huge diamond ring that sparkled on the lady's finger. 'Are you flying on your own, madam?' she asked casually, quite sure that none of the diverse mix of travellers that were sitting around her could have been her husband.

'Sadly yes, I lost my husband last year.' She smiled but it didn't reach her eyes.

'Oh, I'm very sorry,' Susan said, unsure what else to say.

'It's fine, he was a fair bit older than me so I always knew I would be on my own eventually, I'd prepared for it a long time ago,' the lady reassured her. She had a serenity that made it seem okay.

Susan thought of Jeff; it had honestly never occurred to her that this would happen to them, she had never thought that far ahead. She shrugged it off quickly, there was absolutely no point in thinking about it, he wasn't *that* old yet!

'Now what sort of film would you like to watch, romance, comedy?' Susan asked with forced brightness.

'Oh, something with a bit of excitement, my dear,' she said, looking up with a twinkle in her eye, so she still had plenty of life left in her, 'and a glass of champagne to watch it with would be wonderful.'

'No problem at all,' Susan smiled back at her. Maybe she would be in this lady's shoes herself one day, and she liked to think she'd have a glass of champagne too.

As she walked back into the galley minutes later David, the flight manager, was standing in front of the entertainment control centre looking baffled, tapping the screen in agitation.

'Everything okay?' Susan asked.

'They've got no screens on down the back, but it says here that everything is fine,' he answered with an air of exasperation, not taking his eyes off the screen.

'Oh dear,' Susan winced. This wasn't good, two hundred passengers without entertainment could make it a difficult flight. 'It's working okay up here,' she offered, trying to cast some hope on the situation. She was relieved that she was, firstly, working in the galley out of sight of the passengers, and secondly in the cabin that did have entertainment, for now at least. She stopped herself from making the 'not my aisle' joke, doubtful that it would be well received at that moment.

'I'm going to have to turn it all off and on again, see if that sorts it out.' David exhaled as he picked up the handset from next to the jumpseat and made an announcement to tell everyone what he was doing, thanking them for their patience. 'Let's hope it works,' he said as he hung up the phone and flipped the switch next to the screen to the OFF position.


Oh, what a flight that had been. The entertainment had not come back on for the rest of the flight. Some sort of remote circuit breaker, the engineers had said when they had boarded in JFK, faced with a crew exhausted from seven hours of entertaining the passengers personally, calming and reasoning with them. It was only their TVs after all, not the engines that were broken, Susan had pointed out on several occasions.

As she closed her hotel door behind her, she stepped out of her heels and sighed loudly as she placed her tired feet flat on the ground. She looked straight ahead through her window that framed the Empire State Building perfectly, oh what a view! The flight hadn't been her favourite of all time admittedly but it was over now, and here she was in New York City with the best view in town.

Opening her suitcase, she took out the bottle of champagne which she had brought with her. It was still chilled from being in the cargo hold, and the sound of the cork popping was the best thing that she had heard all day. She poured the bubbling nectar into the crystal flute that she had also carried, and took her first sip with her eyes closed in order to fully appreciate the moment.

Carrying her designer toiletry bag into the small but modern bathroom, she quickly found the expensive bath oils that she had treated herself to at the weekend, squeezing a few drops into the hot water that was now flowing from the faucet. In just a few minutes Susan lay in luxury, imagining that she was in an exclusive spa, breathing in the aromas of the oils that were worth every penny of their expensive price tag. For the next twenty minutes she only moved to sip her champagne.

Stepping out of the bath that was beginning to cool now, revitalised, she dried herself gently with the fluffy white towel. She smoothed deliciously smelling lotion into her tanned limbs, and applied the creams that promised miracles onto her face. Shaking out her hair from its pins it fell perfectly, if a little tousled, around her shoulders. She glanced at the bedside clock as she opened her case again, 5:15pm. From under her clothes she soon found what she was looking for, taking out the small silk bag. She laid out the contents on the white bed sheets and admired the beautiful red lace underwear, before putting it on and standing in front of the mirror. A quick brush of bronzer on her face, and slick of lip gloss, and she was ready, just in time. The sound of the key card in the door made her smile, and when he came into the room she was soon lifted off her feet, her legs wrapped around his lean muscular body as he carried her to the bed without saying a word.

# Chapter 3

Susan Harrison held on to the arm of Tony Carluccio as they walked along Broadway, letting him lead her through the throngs of people. Tall and broad, he was the epitome of the American Italian, thick dark wavy hair and olive skin. At thirty years old he was younger than her, but he had never asked her age, and it didn't matter; she knew that they looked good together, and whenever she was with him he made her feel like she was the most beautiful woman in the world. She felt like she was walking on air.

They had first met two years ago, him being the newly appointed manager at the crew's hotel in New York. She had always thought since that he was wasted in hotels, he should've been on TV with his looks and charm.

He had come to her room that night to check out a broken tap, and hadn't left for over an hour; he had never fixed the tap. Now he came to her room every time she was in the city, and for those twenty-four hours she was in town, when he wasn't working, she was 'his girl' and he was 'her man'.

There were rules of course, she had had to set them at the beginning, just in case things got complicated. It was purely a fling, that would last as long as they both wanted it to, there would be no commitment. He wasn't to ask about her other life, about Susan Kennedy, she was no one to him. She wouldn't be meeting his parents, or going to family parties, she would be with him alone when she was here, he was the only one that she needed to see. Nor was he to contact her, she would contact him, when she was coming to town, and only then. Tony was fine with all of that, happy even; no ties but all the good bits, it seemed that it suited him perfectly.

Tonight he was taking her to a show, and she felt giddy as they walked there; perhaps it was the champagne, or maybe it was the after-effects of the way he had made her feel back there in the hotel room. She squeezed his arm and looked up at him, feeling the intensity of his stare as he looked back at her all through her body. The show would be great but, if she was honest, she couldn't wait to get back to the hotel afterwards, to be back in that room with him. The excitement of having to sneak in separately so that his colleagues, or hers for that matter, didn't see them together added to her butterflies, and she drew a deep breath of air trying to calm them.

The next afternoon Susan put her lipstick on and tied her scarf, checking herself in the mirror by the door. She smoothed down her dress and stood upright, looking at the perfectly groomed flight attendant that was looking straight back at her. Tony had left for work that morning and she was ready to go home now, reenergised and rejuvenated. Pulling her suitcase and crew bag behind her, she took the elevator down to the ground floor. She walked purposely across the lobby towards the crew that were huddled together, trying not to look at him behind the desk. He was talking to the receptionist but she could tell that he was watching her at the same time.

'Did you have a nice trip?' asked Sam, one of the crew that she had been working with on the flight out.

'Yes, thanks, hon, did you?' She was glad of the conversation, of the distraction.

'Yeah, lovely, lots of shopping. Shame you didn't make last night, we all went to the roof bar at 230 Fifth, you were the only one who didn't come.' She was looking at Susan for an explanation, for a reason why she had been so unsociable.

'Oh, I was really tired, I just fell asleep after I had a bath,' she lied. 'That's a shame though, I would have loved that. Definitely next time I'm here,' she lied again.

'I get it, sometimes you just have to catch up on your sleep,' Sam said understandingly.

Susan nodded. Truth was she had had very little sleep at all, but she didn't feel tired now, and there would be plenty of time to catch up when she was at home.

'Bus is here,' announced the captain, walking towards their group, retrieving his case from the untidy collection of them and leading the way out of the door.

'Thank you,' Susan said to the bellman who was holding the door open, looking back over her shoulder to check that Tony was still watching her, pleased to see that he was.

Susan Kennedy landed in London the next morning, home now for the week. As she switched on her phone a message from Jeff popped up on the screen.

*Welcome home, we missed you.*

*That's nice*, she thought, dropping her phone back into her bag and taking out a small black pouch. From inside she retrieved two rings, sliding them back onto her wedding finger and admiring the sparkle of the diamonds for a moment. Susan Kennedy was home.

# Chapter 4

'Mum, I missed you!' Lewis cried as he hugged her unashamedly in the playground.

'I missed you too, honey,' she said, hugging him tightly back.

'Hi, Mum.' Sophia walked up behind them and gave her mum a much more understated and quicker hug. Susan missed her little girl, who didn't care about what the others thought, but she remembered being ten once, and trying to be one of the cool kids. No one wanted to be one of the nerds after all, although she wondered if Lewis would ever actually care.

'Shall we go out for tea?' She knew the answer already.

'Yes,' they both said eagerly.

She didn't feel like cooking tonight, and she knew that Jeff wouldn't mind if she brought him home something nice from Chimichangas, the kids' favourite place for dinner.

As they drove home from the restaurant later, Lewis chatted excitedly to her about his upcoming drama play, in which he had the main part. Sophia was much quieter, taking selfies on her phone in the quest for the perfect Instagram picture. She wished her daughter would stop growing up, just for a moment, and make the most of her last few years of childhood. The little girl was still in there, there were glimpses of her sometimes, but they were getting fewer and further between.

She turned her car into their road and pressed the control to open the gates. As she drove slowly up their driveway she noticed that Luke, the gardener, must have been, as the trees were sculpted to perfection on either side. Her suspicions were confirmed when she saw him across the lawn tending to some plants, and she lost concentration for a moment as she admired his fine physique, borne of hard work. She shook her head, regaining her composure. Not here, not in this life, Susan Kennedy was good.

Jeff had heard them coming and was standing at the large oak door. Milo and Jack, the family's two black Labradors, came bounding out to greet them and the children giggled as they licked their faces.

'Down, you two,' Jeff called firmly, walking over to relieve Susan of her case. 'Welcome home, my love.' He kissed her warmly on the lips, and she smiled at him. New York was gone now, and Susan Kennedy was happy to be home, with her family.

She followed him up the steps into the house and looked around the generous entrance hall. The house was immaculate as always, and she thanked her lucky stars every day that Jeff had given her a cleaner so that she didn't need to worry about such things. Goodness knew it was hard enough doing all the other things that she did in her role of the perfect wife and mother, without having to clean a house of this size. Not that she would ever complain about its size, of course. With its five suite-sized bedrooms and four bathrooms it was a beautiful and imposing home, and she was very lucky to have it.

'Champagne?' Jeff called from the kitchen. The children had both disappeared already, off to their rooms, their own little kingdoms.

'Of course,' she replied, in a tone that said he needn't have asked. She took off her uniform jacket and hung it on the back of one of the barstools that sat at the large, quartz-topped island which stood central to the huge kitchen. 'You know me too well, my dear.'

He handed her a glass, which she took gratefully. Jeff didn't really drink himself, but he never minded that she did, personally buying her the best champagne and making sure it was always chilled and ready should she want a glass or four.

'How was your flight?' he asked eagerly, obviously pleased to have her back and wanting to listen to anything she had to tell him.

'Oh, it was brilliant, I went to a gorgeous rooftop bar with the crew in the evening, such a lovely place. It had the most amazing views of the Empire State Building.' She had to be careful, had to make her trips sound like this. If she was to say she had done nothing and just slept then he would question why she wouldn't leave, it was certainly not like she needed to work after all. She had already been in the job before she met him though, and so he couldn't force her to leave something she loved this much, not that he hadn't tried.

'Sounds lovely, maybe we should go there together one

day, you could show me around.'

'Yes, maybe we should,' she agreed, knowing that it would, and could, never happen.

'So, Andy and Evelyn are coming tomorrow night at seven, is that okay?'

Susan drank the last of the champagne in her glass before looking up with her smile fixed.

'Absolutely, I'm really looking forward to it. Any ideas what you would like for dinner?'

'No, surprise me, you always pull something extraordinary together.' He topped up her glass and kissed her head. She knew what tonight was bringing and she hoped that the champagne would help.

As Jeff wrapped her in his arms after he had made love to her she knew she had done her job well, he was happy. She tried to ignore the repulsion that she was starting to feel as she watched his waistline growing, his stomach pressing against her back now. She wondered if perhaps she needed to encourage him to get back into exercise and stop eating those big lunches in the city when he was at work. Surely ageing didn't need to be unattractive?

# Chapter 5

The next morning Susan took the children to school and drove straight to the M&S food hall. She glided around the aisles with her shopping trolley, selecting the food she would need for their dinner that evening. She would spend the day preparing a banquet, and Susan Kennedy was never happier than when she was at home in the kitchen creating something spectacular.

Three hours later the kitchen was in turmoil, every pan used, and she was relieved when her loyal cleaner, Lucy, set about restoring order. Middle-aged and plain looking, Lucy had been a godsend to Susan these past five years.

'Would you mind picking the kids up for me, Lucy, so that I can get ready?' Susan asked when she noticed that it was nearly time for them to finish school. Lucy was much more than a cleaner to her, she was a driver, a PA, an *enabler*; the one who enabled her to be as great a wife as she was. If she'd had to go out now she would never have got the desserts finished, or herself ready in time.

'No problem,' Lucy replied, taking the keys for the Range Rover from the side. Susan suspected that she was quite happy to get out of the house for a bit, and to drive the car that she could probably only dream of driving in her own life, and she was happy to give her the opportunity. She hadn't forgotten that she didn't come from this kind of life herself, not everyone was as lucky as her.

That evening, as she sat at the table making small talk with Evelyn, the men droned on about business. They were both the same age as Jeff, and Susan struggled to talk to Evelyn as a peer, and not feel like she was talking to her mother. Of course, Evelyn would never have guessed that she was struggling, Susan was too good to let her true feelings show. Years of flying had given her the skill of making conversation with almost anyone, no matter how little they had in common.

'I just need to check on the children,' she excused herself. She hadn't seen them since she had fed them pizza at five o'clock and bribed them with a day out tomorrow if they were good tonight. Like children from a bygone age, they were to be seen and not heard.

Lewis was absorbed in his game when she snuck in behind him. 'Behind you,' he cried to someone through his headset. On the screen in front of him figures in battle clothes ran around shooting each other. Susan wasn't sure he should be playing the game at his age, but all of his friends were so she couldn't make him the odd one out. He turned and gave her a quick wave and one of his huge smiles, turning back around quickly and pressing the buttons on his controller furiously. She stood in the doorway for a moment, watched her little boy in his little world, and felt her heart swell with the love that she felt for him. He really did light up her life with his big smile and happy ways.

Along the hallway Sophia was lying on her king-sized bed, headphones in, fairy lights twinkling around the vast room. She was such a lucky girl, Susan would have loved a room like this at her age, with its ensuite bathroom, walk-in wardrobe and sofa. What other little girls had space for a sofa in their bedroom? She wondered if Sophia really appreciated it though, if she told her often enough how lucky she was? These were just things to her, things that she was used to. She sat on the bed and her daughter turned around and gave her a smile that melted her, not removing her headphones though, and turning back to her laptop. Her firstborn was a kind and sensitive thing, and she was growing into a formidable young lady. Susan was looking forward to the day when her daughter grew up into her best friend.

Contented and feeling renewed by the brief time with her babies, Susan went back to the dinner table, ready to continue the façade, to entertain them all. It was a just a small part of her full-time job as his wife, and it paid very well. If all she had to do was this to give her and her children their wonderful life, she would do it forever, it wasn't that hard. The evening turned out to not be that bad too, enough wine blurred the differences between them, and animated the boring.

As she and Jeff waved their guests off at the front door, he put his arm around her and held her close. Maybe the passion for him had gone, but she did love him, he was a good husband and a good father, that was undeniable. She looked up and accepted his kiss and his gratitude for her work this evening, going back into their beautiful home together, man and wife.

# Chapter 6

The following Saturday morning Susan packed her case ready for her flight to Miami. She had enjoyed the week, had looked after her family, been to the school play, taken the kids to the theme park, helped them with their homework, tended to Jeff.... the list went on and she needed a bit of 'me time' now. Jeff's parents were coming to stay and she was secretly pleased to be going away, finding them even a little too much for *her* acting ability; their snootiness had lost any filters as they both approached eighty.

'I'm off,' she called loudly from the hall as Jeff carried her small case down the stairs. She heard the footsteps thundering along the landing as one of the kids came running to say goodbye. Sophia ran to her and this time, with no friends around, gave her the biggest hug she'd had from her for a long time.

'Love you, darling, help Daddy with your grandparents.' She looked down at her daughter, who rolled her eyes and grimaced. She was a good girl though and knew how to behave. Just like her mum, she would put on the smile and say the right things, Susan had never knowingly taught her these skills but perhaps she was even more astute than she gave her credit for. Lewis appeared at the top of the stairs, headset on and controller in hand, still in his pyjamas.

'Bye, Mum,' he called, blowing her a kiss, obviously desperate to get back to his game. She blew him kisses back.

'Make sure he's not on that all day,' she said to Jeff, knowing that her husband would happily let them stay on their devices all day long if it meant peace and quiet for him.

'Well you could stay home with us and do something nice together.' He looked at her, raising his eyebrows.

'Jeff!' *Every bloody time*.

'Sorry.' He always said sorry, but he never stopped trying. She kissed him goodbye and turned to the door.

Anyway, he could say what he liked, she thought as she drove her car through the gates, it would take far more than little digs here and there to make her leave her job. She hadn't been to Miami for weeks and couldn't wait to be on South Beach with a cocktail.


Susan Harrison giggled with the other girls in the galley. The huge American football players that were squeezed into the business class seats were making the plane so much more attractive than usual. Even the manager, Julie, who must have been fifty but was extremely glamorous still, was reapplying her lipstick before going out to do drinks. With so many crew at Osprey Aviation it was rare to fly with many crew you knew, but Susan knew Julie Margot, and there was no way she would be going out on a drinks round if the plane was not full of fitties.

'Right, I'm ready,' grinned Julie, pushing out her ample

chest. 'Who's coming with me?'

Susan stepped out of the way to let one of the younger girls jump on the end of Julie's cart; she didn't need the attention today. Twenty minutes later they returned to the galley triumphant, Julie waving a piece of paper in the air.

'Right, I hope you girls have packed some nice clothes because tonight we are going out!'

'Oh my God, really, where are we going?' exclaimed Steph, who had stayed in the galley with Susan.

'Some club on South Beach.' Julie was still waving the piece of paper. 'Guest list, drinks, the works, it's their team night out, lucky us!'

'That's so cool, I can't wait,' said Steph excitedly.

'She was so good out there, a proper pro,' said the girl who had gone out with her. Susan still hadn't got everyone's names yet.

As they all swapped room numbers in the hotel lobby the girls were obviously excited about the night out. Only the two male flight deck were not going, and Susan.

'I can't believe you're not coming out,' Julie said as she passed her on her way to the lift.

'I'm sorry, I just feel a little under the weather so I'm going to try and sleep it off.'

'Okay, love, but if you change your mind we are meeting in my room in an hour,' and she was gone, leaving a waft of expensive perfume behind her.

Susan Harrison knew she looked good, even amongst the glamorous crowds on South Beach. The sound of the sea lapping against the expanse of white sand was slowly being drowned out by the music from the neon lit bars up ahead. She walked purposefully, enjoying the way the ocean breeze blew her short dress against her body, and her hair flowed behind her.

Arriving at The Clevelanders she climbed up the stone steps. The lights reflected on the pool that was between her and the hotel behind, the cocktail bar sitting on the front of the property next to the beach. He was sitting at the bar with his back to her; she would recognise those broad muscular shoulders anywhere. She slowed her pace as she approached him, in case he heard her, and placed her hands teasingly over his eyes.

Mario turned and gave her his broadest, sexiest smile, grabbing her around the waist with his huge hands. She felt tiny when she was with him.

'I missed you, baby,' he said in his sexy American accent. Susan put both of her arms around his neck and kissed him. She wouldn't say that she missed him back, that would mean there were feelings outside of this agreement, but she was definitely pleased to see him.

# Chapter 7

Mario was as dreamy as she remembered, she hadn't seen him for so long. She had met him on a flight several years ago now, and just like today's flight, he had invited all of the girls out to his nightclub. It seemed that he had only had eyes for Susan though, and she had accepted his attentions willingly. Now, whenever she came to Miami, he would be waiting for her, always at The Clevelanders, always with that beautiful smile of his. Somewhere in his family he had a Hispanic heritage, and it showed in his gorgeous black eyes and tanned skin. But she had never seen a Mexican of his size, with such muscles before. The rules were the same, this was just a fling that would last as long as they both wanted it to. She was sure that one day she would message him to say she was coming to Miami and he would tell her that he had a girlfriend, but he hadn't yet so here they were, again.

The cocktails flowed and so did the intensity, it was as if they were the only two in the bar.

'I'll be back in a minute,' he excused himself with a hungry kiss. She didn't ask where he was going, Mario always knew someone, had to make a call, or maybe he just needed the bathroom. She was a little relieved at having a few minutes to compose herself though, to take a deep breath and just enjoy the setting without the undercurrent of energy. Perhaps too, if he hadn't got up then she wouldn't have heard the wails of the crew laughing as they strolled along the beach in front of the bar. Susan ducked, hoping that they wouldn't see her.

'Right, just one in here and then we'll go to the club.'

She heard Julie's voice giving the girls their orders, and the giggles getting closer. She grabbed her drink, and without turning around walked quickly towards the restrooms on the far side. She was sure that no one would have recognised her from the back; it was hard enough from the front sometimes, they all looked so different out of uniform.

She watched, amused, from her safe spot behind a palm tree as Julie passed them all shots, making sure that they were all loosened up and ready to perform once they were at the club. The flight home was going to be a challenge with a full crew hungover!

Mario appeared from a door on her right, hanging up a call on his phone. She waved to him, trying to look casual as she hid behind the tree, and a look of amused confusion flashed across his face.

'What's up?' he smiled as she grabbed his arm and pulled him away.

'Nothing, I just can't wait to get you back to yours.'

He didn't argue, walking around the corner and hailing a cab to take them to his penthouse apartment overlooking the marina.

\* \* \*

Susan was glad she had had the foresight to put a small beach dress in her handbag as she walked back into the hotel lobby the next day and bumped straight into Julie Margot at the coffee bar by the entrance. Her manager's hair was perfect as always but she didn't look quite as groomed as usual and her big sunglasses were hiding her eyes.

'Good night?' Susan asked knowingly.

'Oh amazing, you really missed some fun. Are you feeling better today?'

'Oh yes, much better thanks, just the trip I needed. So how did it go? Did everyone make it home?'

'Oh, you know how these nights go.' That was all the information Susan was going to get, and she did know.

'Two black coffees.' The barista handed Julie the two cups and Susan raised her eyebrows. Julie just smiled, without a flash of embarrassment. Not another word was said as they walked to the lift.

'See you at checkout,' said Julie as she got out on the fifth floor, with her two drinks.

'Yep, see you then,' smiled Susan, stifling her giggles.

# Chapter 8

It was early, a little after eight, and Luke was in the garden again as Susan drove into her driveway. Landing days were always a struggle, as the line between Susan Kennedy and Susan Harrison was somewhat blurred. By tomorrow she would be able to look at him without these feelings that he stirred, but today it was probably best that she avoided him. Perhaps she needed to look at rescheduling him to come in on days other than landing day, for her own sanity.

She groaned when she saw the black Bentley parked in front of the house signalling that her in-laws were still in situ, having hoped that they would be gone by now. It had been a hard flight home, with a full crew performing below par making each service a little more of a struggle, and she had no energy left for these two.

The dogs ran out to meet her, followed by the children, ready for school in their uniforms, Jeff coming behind them all to take her bags.

'I'm so glad you're home, Mum, I can't take much more,' Sophia said quietly as she hugged her. 'Grandma's been driving me mad.'

'Oh dear, don't worry, I'm back now,' Susan soothed, somewhat amused by her daughter's own feelings about them.

'Mum and Dad insisted on staying to see you,' Jeff apologised. Even he knew that his parents could be overbearing, and there was no denying that they looked down on Susan. Even though they had now been married for so long, and with two children, she knew that they still thought she was a gold digger and after their son's money. Perhaps in some ways they weren't wrong, but she wouldn't have stayed with just any rich man, she did love Jeff, it was just that the money made it more appealing and easier. And besides, she worked hard in this marriage, looking after him and their children, putting herself second to their needs all of the time that she was home.

'You look tired, Susan,' said Margaret as she walked into the hall. She was smiling, but Susan knew that it was fake. Her pink lipstick and rouged cheeks added colour to the aged face, a string of pearls and neat bobbed hair setting her into the rich old lady category perfectly.

'Oh, hello, Margaret, how lovely to see you. You're looking well.' Susan ignored her comment, she was better than that. She walked over and air-kissed her cheek.

Jeff's father, George, shuffled through from the dining room. His nose seemed to have got bigger and redder since the last time Susan had seen him, testament to his love of a good single malt whisky.

'George, lovely to see you, how are you?' Of the two he was the easier to like.

'Can't complain, not too bad, thank you.'

'I'm so pleased that I got to see you both, I thought I was going to miss you.' She had hoped that she would, anyway.

'No, no, we couldn't have had that. Anyway, let's get you some coffee, you look like you need it,' said Margaret, leading them through to the kitchen.


'So, Susan, when are you going to give up this awful job?' asked Margaret as she passed her a coffee minutes later. 'It's not very becoming of the wife to someone in Jeff's position to be serving people, you know.'

Susan was speechless, despite the fact that this certainly wasn't the first time Margaret had expressed her opinion on the matter. The three of them were looking at her, waiting for her response, and she looked at Jeff pleadingly, hoping he would come to her defence, but he didn't.

'Oh, Margaret, you all know I love my job, I couldn't possibly give it up.'

'But you don't need to work, Susan, my son provides for you all and takes care of you.'

'I know he does.' Susan could feel the anger rising as they all stared at her; how dare they bully her, and on landing day of all days. 'And I look after them all very well too, Margaret.' It was a two-way contract, how dare she suggest otherwise.

'Well I think you are very selfish, leaving them like you do, you should be here.'

'Mother.' Finally Jeff stepped in, and Susan was so relieved to have an ally. 'Susan knows I would like her to stay home too but she has her own mind and won't budge so I can't force her.'

Susan stood up; that was it! He wasn't her ally, he was making it worse.

'Anyway, Jeff, are you taking the children into school before you go to work?' She had to end this conversation before she lost her composure.

'Oh yes, is that the time?' He looked down at his Rolex.

'We may as well leave with you, son,' said George, 'let Susan get some rest.'

'Well it was lovely to see you both,' she lied, speaking through gritted teeth, 'please come back very soon.'


She waved everyone off from the front steps, relieved beyond words that they were gone. Her anger still bubbled below the surface, and she slipped on some flat shoes, summoning the dogs to walk around the garden with her to get some fresh air. It was a beautiful late September day, and she breathed in deeply, feeling instantly better. She walked down past the pool that was covered up now for the autumn, and towards the summer house, watching the two dogs jumping around playfully without a care in the world.

The summerhouse was her retreat, the place she escaped to when she needed to pull a face or let out a scream, a bit like the galley on the plane. She went in and reclined on the cream couch, closing her eyes for a moment. She must have fallen asleep, the knocks on the window confusing her dreams, and she lay for a moment trying to work out where in the world she was.

'Sorry, I didn't mean to wake you,' said Luke, standing in the door, a vision of beauty.

Susan Harrison didn't mind Luke waking her at all.

# Chapter 9

She'd crossed the line, she'd lost control. Susan was furious with herself. Of course, she knew what had happened, she had forgotten where she was for that moment, still in her uniform, woken from her dreams of faraway places. She couldn't remember what had been said, or not said, that had moved them from her being woken to the delicious encounter that they had just had. She couldn't deny that she had enjoyed it, that she wanted more, but not here, not in this life!

The others were easy, she left them in their cities far away, with Susan Harrison, and there were rules. Here though she must be Susan Kennedy, and Susan Kennedy couldn't do things like this, she had far too much to lose. It must never happen again! She stood under the water that pulsated from the shower, washing it away, controlling her breathing, putting it in perspective. She could always fire Luke, that would make things easier, but it wasn't his fault. No, she would just avoid him from now on, *especially on landing day.*

As she walked around the food aisle hours later she

knew that she needed to be amazing tonight. To be the best wife, to prove to Jeff, but more so to herself, that she was as good as she knew that she was. That little blip wouldn't happen again. She swiped away the memories of the morning's encounter with Jeff and his parents; they would never change, nor would he ever give up on getting her to leave her job. But if she could just maintain her perfection at home then she could justify her breaks to herself more easily.

Jeff wrestled with the front door, she could hear him from the kitchen. The children had been fed and were both in their rooms, as it was past seven o'clock after all. She had made an extra effort tonight, even down to the underwear that she knew he would like. Her dress fit perfectly, showing off her figure, and despite being in the house she would keep the designer heels on for the evening.

A huge bouquet of flowers came through the kitchen door first, hiding her husband behind them, so no wonder he had had trouble opening the front door. The purple tissue paper rustled as he struggled with carrying his briefcase and them, and she moved quickly to relieve him of his load.

'Jeff they are beautiful,' she sighed, feeling quite humbled.

'And so are you.' Jeff looked at her admiringly before pulling her to him and kissing her. 'I needed to say sorry for my parents, well my mother, God she was awful to you this morning.'

Susan couldn't disagree, taking the flowers to the sink without saying anything.

'I know I give you a hard time about your job, but I

shouldn't have let them. I've been thinking about it all day, I'm sorry I didn't fight your corner for you.'

'Apology accepted,' she said softly; she couldn't say that it was okay, because it wasn't. Perhaps if had supported her she wouldn't have gone in the garden, and she wouldn't have slept with Luke. Perhaps a little bit of it was his fault. She felt somewhat better sharing the blame with him, not that he had any idea.

'Something smells wonderful.' He wrinkled his nose.

'Beef Wellington, my love,' she announced.

'My favourite.' He was pleased, she could tell.

'I know,' Susan replied matter-of-factly as she helped him off with his jacket and gestured for him to sit at the table that she had laid for two.

'If you spoil me like this you can't wonder why I hate you being away.'

'Sssh,' she said, pouring herself a glass of champagne before taking the food from the oven. 'Just enjoy being spoiled.'

'No arguments here.'

Jeff looked so relaxed and happy as they sat and ate dinner together. He got animated as he told her about his experience on the underground that day, and she laughed. She had always loved his sense of humour, it was how he had first got her to go on a date with him. She hadn't known then that he was rich, and she wouldn't have cared if he wasn't, he was gorgeous and funny and back then that was all that had mattered to the twenty-two-year-old her. She doubted that they would have stayed together so long in poverty though, suspecting that she would have got bored.

As they enjoyed each other's company she felt guilty

about Luke. She had never felt guilty before, but this was different, it was at their home, and she couldn't feel good about it. With the guilt came compassion for this wonderful man who had promised to love her 'until death us do part', and when she told him she loved him that night she meant it more than she had for a long, long time.

# Chapter 10

'I think we should all have a holiday, Jeff, we haven't had a family holiday for ages,' Susan said as she made his coffee the next morning. Jeff was still dopey-eyed from their night together, and she suspected that he would give her just about anything she asked for right now. It was true though, he was working long hours, and they hadn't been away together for a long while. She would love to spend some quality time with the children before they grew up any more.

'Great idea, where are you thinking?'

'How about Dubai? It's half term soon, we could go then.'

'Anything you want, book it up, just let Janice know the dates so she can arrange my diary.' Janice was his PA, and was as invaluable to Jeff as Lucy was to Susan.

'You are wonderful, thank you.'

'I know, don't you forget it,' he quipped as he put on his jacket. Susan loved that his old self was still in there beneath the ageing man, and she waved him off from the door with a smile on her face, a real smile.

As she turned to go back in, the gates opened again

and Luke's small yellow van drove through them, so she quickly ran inside and closed the door. What the hell had she been thinking? Risking all of this for a boy in a yellow van?!

Susan parked her car at the school and walked the children into the playground. Sophia ran off straight away, a little embarrassed by her mum's choice of bright gym wear. Lewis, however, stayed stoically by her side, he wouldn't care if she wore a sack. Anyway, it was designer gym wear and she was going straight to the gym, so quite why her daughter was embarrassed was beyond her.

The bell rang and she waved them both off, turning back to her car. The gym was her only outlet at home, the only time she took for herself, pretty much her only social life. She didn't really have any close friends anymore, getting married so young to someone so removed from her own world had cut most of her ties, but she didn't mind. There was a group of nice ladies in her classes that she would work out with, sometimes going for coffee after, or inviting each other to barbecues and so forth, and that was enough for her. If she had close friends it would mean being open and honest, because that's what close friends did, and she couldn't imagine telling anyone the whole truth about her life. Susan wasn't a worrier though, she didn't worry about things that might or might not happen in the future. She suspected that one day she would tire of the flings and settle more, and maybe then she would let people get a little closer, open up a bit more.

* * *

'Hey, Susan,' called Martha, setting up her equipment in the fitness studio. Susan walked over and put her bag down against the wall behind her. Martha was about the same age as her, with a similar life, her husband albeit a little younger than Jeff.

'Hi.' Susan laid a mat next to her.

'Been anywhere nice lately?'

'Actually, Miami,' Susan said. No one judged her here for her job. They were all wealthy, few of them worked, but their husbands were all too busy working and earning the money for them to travel a fraction of the amount that she did.

'Oh wow, that must have been lovely,' Martha sighed.

'Oh, it was.' That was all that she was prepared to say.

A pretty blonde girl she hadn't seen before had laid a mat down next to her, and Susan turned to introduce herself.

'Susan, this is Laura, she joined last week when you were away.' Martha got in there first.

'Hi, Laura, nice to meet you,' Susan smiled.

'You too,' she smiled back. 'You must be the flight attendant with the beautiful house.'

Susan looked at Martha with raised eyebrows, amused that she'd been the subject of conversation whilst she was away.

'Yes, that'll be me,' she laughed. Martha looked a little embarrassed.

'Martha was telling me all about your garden, I mentioned we were looking for a gardener. We've just moved into the area and the old place is a bit overgrown.'

'Oh, I see.' Now she understood a little better how she had come up in conversation. 'Yes, Luke, he does a fab job, I can give you his details if you like?'

'That would be amazing, thank you.'

Susan was more than happy to give Luke's number out, as hopefully he would get so busy elsewhere he would have to leave his job with her. She could hope.

When she returned from the gym the yellow van was still there, Lucy's mini parked next to it. She quickly jumped out of the car and ran into the house. She wondered how long she could keep this awkwardness up, maybe she would have to speak to him.

In the safety of her house, as he rarely came inside, she climbed the stairs to her suite for a shower. Never as she grew up could she have imagined that her bedroom would one day be the same size as the footprint of her childhood home. Lucy had obviously been in, her sumptuous oversized bed made perfectly. A dressing room lay off to one side, walls lined with bags and shoes, rails of clothes hung in order. The ensuite bathroom was a spa in itself, with its whirlpool bath and wet room, towels rolled neatly and toiletries organised perfectly. She walked over to the bedroom window, gazing out over the garden down to the fields that lay behind, appreciating everything that she had.

Her stomach knotted when she saw the two of them, standing too close to each other, deep in conversation, Luke and Lucy. She had never seen them talk before, and her mind whirred as she imagined what they were saying. Surely, they weren't friendly enough for him to tell Lucy about the summer house? Susan felt the panic rising, breathing deeply and trying to talk herself down. *You are just being paranoid*, she told herself, *because of what you did*. It worked a little bit, her heart rate slowing some, but she couldn't quite accept it. She watched them, she thought she saw him gesture in the direction of the summer house, and they talked for several minutes more before Lucy turned and walked back to the house.

She couldn't live like this, feeling out of control, her world at risk. Something would have to be done.

# Chapter 11

'Hi, Lucy, how are you today?' Susan asked casually as she walked into the kitchen, showered and ready to tackle the problem.

'Fine thank you, and yourself?'

Was there an undertone? Was she speaking to her differently? Susan called on all of her senses to work out if Lucy knew anything.

'Oh, pretty good, I had a great work out this morning. I can see you've been busy in the house, I really don't know what I'd do without you.' She made eye contact with her and held it so that she could read her better.

'You're too kind. I dare say you'd manage fine without me, it's just a lot of rooms to clean, that's all,' Lucy said kindly. Susan started to relax, Lucy was being perfectly normal.

'I don't know about that,' she disagreed light-heartedly, turning away to fill the coffee machine with beans. 'Lucy, is everything okay with Luke? I saw you talking to him in the garden earlier and he looked concerned.' She turned back quickly to see what reaction was provoked on her face, but couldn't read it.

Lucy stalled, seemingly unsure, before going on. 'It was nothing, no, he's fine, we were just having a chat.'

Susan's heart was beating faster; so there *was* something. Lucy looked sad almost, but not accusing, she didn't feel that she knew anything about what had happened between them. 'Oh, I didn't know that you knew Luke that well, I don't think I've ever seen you two talking before. You're always inside and he's always outside!' she said, trying her best to sound casual.

'Oh, no, he's my nephew, my sister's son. It was me who recommended him to your husband, I thought you realised that?' Lucy was obviously surprised that she never knew the connection.

'No, no I never knew that,' Susan said slowly, quite shocked. Luke had just appeared one day last summer, replacing the old man who used to come. She knew Jeff had found him by recommendation whilst she'd been away, but never realised it was through Lucy. *Well, well*, she thought, *now that's all news to me.*

'Yes, him and his girlfriend have just had a baby,' Lucy went on.

'A new baby, how lovely,' Susan said. That was welcome news, Luke had as much to lose as her, well almost, by letting their indiscretion get out. Susan felt the weight lift off her shoulders and a smile spread across her face.

'Yes, a beautiful little girl, but his girlfriend is struggling a bit, and poor Luke is taking the brunt of it.'

'Oh dear, hopefully she'll feel better soon,' *and keep Luke happy*, Susan finished the sentence in her head.

'I'm sure she will, it's just a bit of post-natal. Anyway, I'm off to do the bathrooms, anything specific you need from me today?'

'No thank you, Lucy, you always know exactly what needs doing.'

Susan sipped her coffee, deep in thought. She was positive that Luke hadn't told Lucy anything, and now knowing about his family she was quite sure that he wouldn't. No, he was just a man, happy to have a one-night stand, or one-afternoon stand anyway. It was a shame he didn't live abroad, maybe they'd have had a fling, but not here. She felt lighter, able to put it all in perspective now.

Susan put down the phone to her travel consultant. She had told him exactly what her requirements were for their holiday and he had just called her straight back with his recommendation, which she had taken happily; business class travel, October 23rd, seven nights in a family suite at The Atlantis. She had always wanted to stay there, and the children would love it with its aquarium and water park onsite.

She picked up the phone and dialled the number for Jeff's office in Canary Wharf. She wasn't quite sure exactly what it was Jeff did, something to do with other people's money. He had tried to explain it to her many years ago, on landing day, and she had fallen asleep. He had never tried again since, even when she had asked, pretending to be offended, but she knew that he wasn't really. When he put on that jacket in the morning he was going to his world, just like she did when she went to work; well, maybe not quite the same!

'Kennedy Holdings,' Janice's voice grated on Susan.

'Hi, Janice, it's Susan.'

'Oh, good afternoon, Mrs Kennedy, what can I do for you?'

Grrr, what was with the stuck-up cow? Susan always used her first name, and she would never use it back. She had been Jeff's PA for years now, since she had Lewis, so eight, and had always been so frosty. Of course, she was indispensable to Jeff so he wouldn't hear a bad word about her, and it wasn't like she had to socialise with her so she had to just let it go.

'Jeff asked me to let you know the dates for our holiday so that you could plan his diary. Please can you keep him free from October 23rd until the 30th?'

'Certainly. Is there anything else I can do for you, Mrs Kennedy?'

'No thank you, Janice.'

'Goodbye then.' Click, and she was gone.

Susan looked at the phone and rolled her eyes; what a delight *she* was.


'I've booked the holiday,' Susan called down the stairs when she heard Jeff coming in. She was supervising showers between the children's rooms, not quite trusting Lewis not to flood the bathroom quite yet.

'Fabulous, where are we staying?' he called back up.

'The Atlantis.' Susan couldn't hide the excitement in her voice, now standing at the top of the stairs, hoping he would be just as pleased.

He looked back up at her, smiling broadly. 'Sounds great, I had better try and lose some of this before I have to get my body out.' He rubbed his tummy.

'Well it wouldn't hurt to lose a little,' she teased, secretly hoping that he meant it this time. 'Think of your health.'

'Okay, okay, point taken, diet starts tomorrow,' he said derisively as he walked through to the kitchen.

# Chapter 12

Things were changing at home, for the better, Susan thought happily as she drove to work. Jeff really had embraced the diet, and started working out again. After all, they had a fully equipped gym that just gathered dust above the double garage, so he had no excuse not to. In just a few days she was starting to see the difference in him, liking it a lot, having to pretend less.

The problem with Luke had just disappeared, it was as if it had never happened. She could even bring herself to acknowledge him now without blushing, and he seemed as keen as her to act like things were completely normal between them, so much so that she was starting to believe that they were.

She felt happy and contented, not so desperate to get away as she had been for a long time now, not needing to switch to Susan Harrison the moment she drove out through the gates. In fact, she might even miss them all this trip, maybe a little. *Perhaps it wouldn't hurt to tell Jeff that*, she thought as she called his number.

'Kennedy Holdings.' *Ugh, Janice.*

'Hi, Janice, it's Susan, can I speak to my husband please?'

'Sorry, Mrs Kennedy, but he is busy right now, he's asked not to be disturbed.'

'Oh okay, can you tell him I called please?'

'Yes, I will do that. Goodbye.' Click.

Susan was speechless; what had she ever done to the uptight cow to make her so horrid? Maybe she would have to start paying some visits to the office soon. Put her in her place.

'Well, good morning, ladies and gentlemen, and a very warm welcome on board this Osprey Aviation flight OS556 to San Francisco.' Susan Harrison realised she hadn't been paying attention in the pre-flight briefing and listened intently to the next part of the announcement. 'The captain informs us that the flight time today will be approximately eleven hours....' She looked at her watch and quickly worked out the landing time, and more importantly, the time she would get to the hotel.

Alone in the rear galley of the Boeing 787 as the safety demonstration played, she dug deep into her handbag, taking out the phone that lived there, the one that never came out in England. She waited for the screen to come on, quickly going to messages.

*Will be ready by 5 xxx,* she typed and pressed send.

*Couldn't come soon enough xxx*

'Naughty, naughty,' teased Darren, the purser, as he walked into the galley; it was strictly forbidden to use your phone on board.

'Oops, glad it was only you,' Susan said, relieved it wasn't the flight manager who had caught her. She hadn't flown with this one before, but judging by her briefing she was a bit of a stickler.

'Haha,' said Darren in his West Country accent. 'I couldn't give a shit, love, but I'd watch 'er if I were you.' He nodded to Fiona walking down the aisle, checking that the passengers were all secure, that the crew had done their checks right. 'We'd better just do things by the book today, or she'll 'ave us all up for a debrief, she loves a debrief she does.'

Susan laughed inwardly, smiling broadly at Fiona as she came into the galley, checking that every latch was down and every brake on, sighing loudly when she found one that wasn't. She knew how to play these ones, they believed they did the job better than everyone else, and so you had to tell them they did, then they could relax, not needing to prove anything anymore.

'Oh, so sorry, Fiona, I must have missed one, good job you're checking. That's why you're the manager.' Not a hint of sarcasm, and the sincerest of faces, despite Darren's pretend vomiting behind her.

'Yes, well you won't miss one next time, will you,' said Fiona, satisfied that her charge had learned her lesson and acknowledged her seniority.

'How could you say that with a straight face? Arse licker,' Darren laughed when she had left.

'Oh, I'm quite good at disguising my true feelings,' Susan replied smugly.


'Flight manager to flight deck.'

Susan wasn't sure if she had heard it right, somewhere between awake and asleep in her crew bunk above the galley. She heard the others moving around, murmurs of confusion, and fumbled around on the sidewall for the button to turn her light on. In all of her years of flying she had only ever heard that announcement on her annual safety training. She quickly pulled on her skirt and shuffled to the end of her bed, waiting for her turn to go down the narrow stairwell and through the door into the galley below.

The lights in the galley made them all squint, and the ones who had just got up rearranged their clothes and tried to come around quicker than they normally would have to. No one was saying much, but Susan could see the looks of concern on their faces; that command was only to be used in an emergency.

They waited for what seemed an age for Fiona to come to the galley, her face now more serious than ever.

'Okay, listen up everybody,' she started, and no one made a sound as she began to deliver the details of the situation. 'There seems to be a problem with one of the engines, and we will be diverting to a military airfield on the east coast of Canada in approximately twenty minutes. The captain intends to make a normal landing, and is presuming that the engine will still be okay by then, he's just not happy to continue all of the way to San Francisco in case it gets worse. There is a chance it is just a faulty reading so please try not to worry.' They all listened intently, and Susan could feel the atmosphere lighten when they realised they weren't about to ditch over the Atlantic. She hoped that she would never have to find out if those slides really did hold as many people at the manufacturers said that they did, whilst riding the waves of the North Atlantic!

'Anyway, let's get the cabin secured, and the galleys,'

Fiona concluded, looking at Susan as she said the last bit.

Susan listened to the captain telling the passengers about the diversion, and that they had absolutely nothing to worry about. Despite his assurances she couldn't help feeling a little emotional, the fact that there might be something wrong with an engine could never be something not to worry about, surely? Most of the time at work she forgot that she was in a metal tube in the sky, but right now the 37,000 feet between her and the ground were very real. She consoled herself with the fact that at least they weren't over the ocean though, that would have been much, much worse!

She closed her eyes for a moment as they made their final descent, wishing away the next few minutes. Her worry wasn't for her, but for her family, especially the children, who needed their mum, and Mum always came back.

# Chapter 13

It was never going to be easy, landing at a military base in the middle of nowhere, with two hundred and fifty passengers and no facilities to talk of. There were also none of their engineers there, and no spare engines funnily enough, so they just sat and waited for updates on what the hell they were going to do.

Even worse, there was no phone signal, no way of getting hold of anyone, to let them know that you were going to be very late. The airline had contacted their loved ones, in case they heard about the diversion and worried, but she could hardly ask them to call the married man that was driving from San Diego to meet her in secret, could she?

Yes, Mark was married, but then so was she, so she could hardly judge him on that count. He was a little older than the others, but she had nothing against older men, just ones that didn't age well. He had only ever mentioned his wife and kids once, the first time that they met in a speakeasy bar in San Francisco, but never since then, and her likewise. The same rules applied with him as with all of the others. She hoped that he had checked to see if her flight was delayed before setting off.

Two hours passed, the passengers strangely accepting of the situation, watching their TVs and taking the drinks that the crew offered them gratefully. If she had imagined how it would play out she would have pictured them all standing up demanding they be taken to their destination immediately, blaming the airline and their incompetence. But it seemed they were all mostly of the same mind, grateful to be in one piece on the ground, that today their number wasn't up.

'I want to speak to the captain,' came the voice from behind her as she stood in the galley with Darren. Well there was always going to be one.

'I'm sorry, sir, but the captain is busy right now, anything I can help you with?' Darren said, all politeness and professionalism.

'I doubt it,' said the unsavoury looking little man that had just come in. 'I doubt you know any more than I do. I have a very important meeting I need to get to and I want to know what the hell the plans are.'

The captain's voice came over the PA, saving Darren the pain of having to deal with this person who was obviously going to be difficult and condescending. Darren held his hand up at him, signalling that he needed to shut up and listen.

'Well please accept my apologies, ladies and gentlemen, we finally have a plan and are hoping to get things moving very shortly. An aircraft is currently being readied in Detroit to come and pick us all up.' A few of the passengers cheered, a little prematurely. 'Unfortunately though, because of duty hours and limitations, the crew on the relief aircraft will be unable to take us all the way to San Francisco, but will be taking us back to Detroit, where we will all be clearing immigration, before catching a domestic flight to our destination.' The cheers were replaced by groans; there was still a very long day ahead. 'We really appreciate your patience, I know you are all as frustrated as we are right now, and I sincerely apologise for the delay, but I do ask that you do *not* in *any* way take your frustrations out on my crew, who I know have done their utmost for you, and are ultimately in the same situation as all of you.'

Darren and Susan couldn't help but look at the man as the captain said the last bit, defying him to make any derisory comments, and he scurried back to his seat. They both huddled behind the galley bulkhead, where no one could see them, knowing that the mood in the cabin would not be great right now. Susan felt sorry for her colleagues who couldn't hide as they sat on their jumpseats opposite passengers at the doors further up, wondering if she should go and relieve them, but deciding against it.

Susan switched her phone on as they landed in Detroit; they should have arrived in San Francisco an hour ago.

*Just landed in Detroit, we had to divert, won't be getting in until midnight now, sorry.* She sent the message, hoping he had known already and not made the journey.

*Oh no. Where shall I meet you?*

Susan looked at the phone. She was tired already and knew that in another six hours even she would struggle to be on form. But he had come to see her and it wouldn't be fair not to see him at all. Would it?

*I think I will be too tired to go anywhere tonight Mark, I'm sorry xxx*

He took a while to reply.

*It's fine, I understand, I'll get a room tonight, how about breakfast tomorrow?*

*Sounds great, Pick me up at 9:30 xxx*

Well that wasn't so hard after all she thought. Mark was probably the most emotional of her beaux, and she had wondered if perhaps he liked her a little too much sometimes, only agreeing to her rules because otherwise he wouldn't see her at all. Anyway, she knew he would always go home to his wife, and she spaced out her trips here enough to stop him getting too attached; thank goodness she was part time and able to move her flights easily enough.

The crew and the passengers landed in San Francisco like something out of a zombie movie, all exhausted from their almost twenty-four-hour adventure. In the hotel Susan climbed into her bed and set her alarm, falling asleep immediately after, glad that she had no one to interrupt her dreams. Tonight's dreams were of home though, of Jeff and the children, and she woke up the next morning feeling a little unsettled that Susan Kennedy had been here, in Susan Harrison's world.

# Chapter 14

Exactly on time Mark's shiny black Chevy drove onto the hotel forecourt. Susan jumped into the passenger seat, giving him a quick kiss and settling into the soft leather seat as he pulled off. The smile on his face told her that he was pleased to see her. She studied him as he drove them along Fisherman's Wharf, noticing that the silver in his hair was starting to spread further. It made him look even more distinguished though, with his chiselled jaw and bright blue eyes. In some ways he reminded her of Jeff, like how she and Jeff would be if they were ever to have a weekend away somewhere beautiful on their own, ever. She couldn't remember such a time since before the children, all there had been were a few family holidays. She left the children enough when she came away, and didn't want to leave them any more than that, so she didn't push for romantic breaks, and he certainly never mentioned having one.

'How about Sausalito?' He turned and smiled at her, the lines that framed his eyes adding to his attraction. 'Let's take the ferry over.'

He turned opposite Pier 39 and parked up, taking her hand as they crossed over to the ferry building. Twenty minutes later they stood on the deck of the ferry, leaning against the railings and taking in the beauty of San Francisco Bay. The morning mist was just clearing from the Golden Gate Bridge, and the sun reflected off its orange steel. They passed Alcatraz, the decaying prison standing on its rock defiantly, tourists snapping away, taking pictures with it. Mark too was taking pictures.

'Come on, let's get a selfie,' he called to her as he pointed the camera at himself with the prison behind. Susan shook her head; that would not be a good idea, why would he even suggest it? What if his wife saw it? He laughed and took the picture of himself, and she was relieved to see that it was just a joke, that he wasn't that indiscreet.

As they sat on the veranda at the back of the restaurant that perched over the water, small waves lapping underneath them, conversation came easily. Susan regaled him with the comedic version of her day yesterday, which was much easier to laugh at now than it had been when she had arrived, almost delirious, the night before. Mark managed to make his job in Silicon Valley sound interesting too, despite it probably being quite boring. He was a people watcher, he saw people's characters and could dissect them, make them funny even if they were the most boring person in the world. He could also read people, which sometimes unnerved her; she didn't want him to see past Susan Harrison, but she suspected that he did, not that he said anything to give it away. The late breakfast turned into lunch, and they both drank champagne. The breath-taking views of the bay were enough to keep them there for hours, getting more and more merry as the afternoon went on, wrapped up in each other's company.

They laughed together on the ferry back as the sun set, and took a taxi to her hotel. Mark knew the rules and followed her in a few minutes later, Susan didn't want to have to explain to anyone who her companion was if she was to bump into any of her crew. Also, it gave her a brief moment to freshen up before the knock came, and she was transported to the realms of pleasure that Mark took her to.

She woke the next morning in Mark's arms, surprised to find that he was still there. Usually he would have left at the crack of dawn, either because he had work, or like today, because it was the weekend and he had family stuff to do, and hadn't he stayed the extra night already?

'Don't you need to get back?' she asked as he put the phone down from ordering room service.

'No, it's Saturday, no work today.'

'What about family stuff?' She hated having to ask, to bring it up.

'Oh,' he hesitated. 'Yeah, we broke up, last month.'

Susan processed what he was saying quickly, trying to decide whether it affected them, this, at all. 'Oh,' was all she could say, pulling away from him and excusing herself to take a shower; was he going to want more from her now?

He was dressed when she came out of the shower, he had obviously felt her shift in energy and seen that it was time to go, clearly not wanting to scare her off.

'Don't worry, I'm not going to go all serious on you, it doesn't change any of this,' he said, looking around him. 'I just like being with you, whenever I can be.'

She smiled at him, relieved, she liked being with him too, every couple of months. She let go of the towel that had wrapped her body away from him. There was no need for him to leave just yet, breakfast was on its way and she had hours until checkout!

# Chapter 15

Well that was close! Susan was pacing up and down in the summerhouse, needing a moment out of sight, trying to get on top of her panic.

Her phone had rung, that was all, but it wasn't her normal phone, *noooo*, it was the *other* phone, the one that she had forgotten to switch off when she had left San Francisco. Bless him, Lewis had thought he had been doing the right thing when he had dug it out of her bag where she had left it in the hall, and run into the kitchen with it.

'Your phone, Mum, it was ringing,' he announced, waving it in the air as she stood telling Jeff about her flight, the edited version.

'Oh, thank you, darling,' she had said calmly, relieved that it had rung off just as he had handed it to her, and that he hadn't noticed that it was a different phone. She had put it down quickly behind the fruit bowl, where Jeff wouldn't see it, wouldn't see that it was a different model to the one he had given her. Thankfully he was just pouring her a landing day fizz so he was distracted, but he *had* heard the ring tone.

'Who was that?' he asked casually. Susan didn't get many calls on Susan Kennedy's phone.

'Oh, probably someone trying to sell me something, I don't recognise the number.'

'You've changed your ringtone though,' he remarked as he passed her the glass, making small talk; she couldn't detect any suspicion in his voice.

'Yes, a moment of boredom. I don't like it though, can't get used to it. I think I'll change it back. So, how's the diet and exercise going?' She had noticed that he was in his workout clothes so he had obviously been at it already this morning, and seized the opportunity to change the subject.

'How do you think?' He smoothed his stomach and flexed his muscles to show her his results.

'I think it's going pretty well.' She nodded approvingly, he was definitely getting leaner, his face was getting more defined. 'Keep up the good work.'

'I will have a beach body for Dubai if it kills me,' he declared. Maybe he had had no reason not to stack on the weight before, perhaps she needed to keep the holidays booked to help him stay motivated. It was possible that she had been a bit selfish; just because *she* was having enough little breaks, perhaps he needed some too. Not like hers though, no, not like hers.

'Right I have to go and send some emails quickly,' he said. 'I'll be in my study if you need me.'

'Okay, love, perhaps we can all go out this afternoon, take the dogs for a run on the downs?'

'Sounds great, get yourself a couple of hours' sleep first though, we don't want you dozing off in the car.' He kissed her forehead and left her sitting there with a pretend look of indignation on her face.

As soon as he was out of sight Susan grabbed the phone and left by the back door. Only when she reached the summerhouse did she look at it. She had never turned it on here before, it was an American phone with an American SIM, for American use! She planned her liaisons from one trip to another, she didn't need to speak or communicate with anyone unless she could see them imminently.

The missed call was from Mark, what the hell? What was so important that he needed to speak to her now? He knew that she didn't contact him unless she was coming to San Francisco; she probably hadn't mentioned that she never turned her phone on at home, or indeed that she had two phones, but surely he would have worked that out? Surely, he was equally as careful? Was she overreacting? It was landing day, after all. There wasn't a voicemail though so she switched it off quickly. There was no way in the world that she was calling him back, he wasn't in her life for the foreseeable, if at all now, she couldn't see someone that was so dangerous, however much she liked them.

As she calmed down she noticed her surroundings, jumping up from the cream couch, remembering the last time that she was in here, with Luke. Had she been naive these past few years to believe she could keep her two lives so separate? Was she walking a dangerous line?

The children ran with the dogs across the downs and they both laughed at them.

'Is it a pack of dogs or a pack of kids?' Jeff asked. Susan

held on to his arm as they walked slowly. She loved these days, just them and the open air. It didn't matter right now if they lived in a big house or a caravan, it wouldn't have changed this picture. Oh, perhaps the dogs may have to be a bit smaller if they lived in a caravan, she thought, amused at her deduction.

'I really can't decide whether the dogs are like kids or the kids are like wild dogs.' Jeff was still musing over his question.

'I think either is true,' she said as she squeezed his arm.

Maybe she was kidding herself when she thought that she stayed mostly for the material things, because that somewhat justified her other life. Maybe she actually stayed because she loved this bit too, the family bit, her children, her husband. All of the other stuff was just what it was, another life, someone else's.

# Chapter 16

It had been a long time since Susan could remember going to work with no one waiting for her at the other end. It made her feel a bit strange, deflated maybe, unexcited. Yes, that was it, there was no excitement, no knowing that she was going to have a marvellous encounter with someone she knew, no gorgeous man or amazing sex. It was only because she had been on standby that she hadn't been able to choose her flight today, make sure that she was going somewhere worthwhile. What on earth was she going to do in Chicago?

Perhaps it wasn't such a bad thing, she thought on the drive to the airport. She had started to wonder if she had some kind of addiction, or at least if Susan Harrison did. She only flew now to places where she knew she had a 'companion.' It was what gave her that buzz when she got in her car and made this drive. But was it stopping her from finding fulfilment in her real life, as Susan Kennedy? When she had a flight lined up she would be distracted, almost wishing the days away until her next 'break', but with only standby looming she hadn't felt like that this week.

She had had a lovely time at home, and now that Jeff was starting to look after himself again he was beginning to stir up her old feelings for him. She would have been quite happy in fact to have stayed at home and not gone to work at all.

She would go out with the crew when she got there, she resolved, do what she used to do before all of the flings had started. She thought back, trying to remember how long ago this had all begun, how it had come to take over her work life. The first had been shortly after she came back from maternity leave, a pilot, but it hadn't lasted long. Others had come and gone, but now she had a steady set, all of whom were very different, and all of whom she liked very much. Despite the deep thoughts and soul searching she wasn't ready to give them up yet, she enjoyed them far too much, and it wasn't hurting anyone as long as everybody stuck to the rules.

As she walked out to her car with her case, Luke was just walking across the front of the house.

'Morning,' he said, stopping her in her tracks.

'Good morning, Luke, how are you?' She didn't really want to know how he was, but she couldn't be rude.

'Not too bad thanks, and thanks for the recommendation.'

Susan had to think for a moment, and he must have seen the puzzled look on her face.

'Laura Mansfield, she said she got my number from you at the gym.'

'Oh, yes.' She had completely forgotten about that. She

made eye contact with him briefly, it wasn't like her to be shy. 'I'm glad she called you, will she be keeping you busy?' She was hopeful.

'Yes, but don't worry, I'll still have time for you, I mean here,' he said cheekily.

*Oh, my word*, she felt the heat rising up her neck, she didn't remember the last time she had felt *embarrassed*. She had thought that things had been forgotten, that it would never be mentioned again!

'Anyway, got to go, I've got a flight to catch,' she said hurriedly. He was grinning at her and she couldn't bear it, throwing her suitcase into the passenger seat and jumping into the car. As she drove down the drive she caught sight of him in the rear-view mirror, just standing there, watching her; it made her feel uneasy. She would have to talk to him when she got back, put him straight on a few things.

The crew check-in area in Heathrow's Terminal 4 was a hive of activity as crew arrived one by one through the glass doors. They would leave through the same doors a short while later, in their new teams, walking to the aircraft together to take their flight. Susan sat relaxed on the sofas in the lounge area, amused by the horrified look on Emma's face as she told her about her last flight and the diversion to Goose Bay.

'Well let's not have any of that today, I'm looking forward to a few drinks at RBs tonight,' said Emma. Susan had flown with her years ago, when they were new, and was relieved to have someone on the crew that wanted to go out and have a good time. The thought of spending the trip on her own had made her feel quite depressed when she had thought it might be a possibility this morning.

'Me too, shame we have to work first,' Susan grinned, and picked up her handbag as their flight was announced, looking around the room as others stood up, obviously their allies for the next few days.

As they came out of the briefing room twenty minutes later everyone was in good spirits. A flight manager could make or break a flight from the offset, but fortunately today Eric was hilarious, bonding them all in their hysteria, line after line of jokes that made Susan's stomach hurt from laughing. They walked out of the door back into the terminal, a new team, chatting excitedly, everyone making their plans for the trip. She glanced behind her quickly to see the smart hats of the three pilots that were joining them. She recognised the captain, with his grey beard and friendly face, walking alongside another nondescript one who would probably turn out to be a nice guy but wasn't attracting much of her interest. The tall, gorgeous one behind them, however, now he had her interest, and he was looking straight back at her.

'Check out our first officer,' Emma nudged her. Susan obviously wasn't the only one who had noticed. 'I wouldn't say no.'

'No, I wouldn't say no either,' Susan replied absent-mindedly.

'Shame you're married, hon. I hope I don't have any other competition amongst these.' Emma signalled to the other girls walking ahead of them. Susan glanced down at her hand, realising that she had forgotten to take off her rings. Plenty of girls would take theirs off for the flight to stop them getting dirty, so she wouldn't be judged for it, and she reached in her bag for the black pouch.

Susan smiled, she wasn't sure whether she was even up for being with anyone this trip anyway, so Emma was probably welcome to him, but being married certainly wasn't a problem, not for Susan Harrison.

# Chapter 17

It had been niggling at her since the other day, and as much as she wanted to ignore it, she couldn't help wondering why Mark had phoned her. She waited for the phone to switch on as she slipped out of her uniform, glad after the long flight to be getting ready to go out, eager to get to the rooftop bar before the sun set. She needed to text Tony, to let him know that she would be in New York shortly anyway, so it wouldn't hurt to see whether Mark had tried to contact her again.

*Ping*

There it was, a message from Mark on her screen. She tried to remember if she had definitely explained the rules to him when she had first met him? Perhaps, having met him in the bar she had forgotten, or he had, and it wasn't like there was a written contract after all, she reasoned.

*Call me when you can xxx*

Ummm, no.

Susan tried not to let her curiosity get the better of her. If it was urgent surely he would have said, and besides she wasn't in San Francisco anytime soon so she didn't need to speak to him. *Perhaps now he has split up from his wife he wants more*, she thought, hoping that that wasn't the case, as it could never happen. She wondered for a moment if she should just block his number, end it there, but then she pictured his handsome face and decided against it. No, she would give him the benefit of the doubt and just explain the rules to him again next time, whenever that would be.

*I'll be arriving on the OS665 on the 15th :) xx*, she texted, giving Tony two weeks' notice; that would be all the information that he needed. She turned the phone off, lest she forget, not wanting a repeat of the last time she did.


'What was going on with immigration and you?' asked Alice, who had been working in the other galley all flight.

They were sitting on deep white sofas on the roof terrace of the bar, just off Michigan Avenue. Chill-out music was playing, cocktails were in hand, and the sun was still warm despite the late month. Susan had long forgotten about immigration, about the vile officer who had looked at her like she was some sort of criminal and sent her to secondary inspection.

Now she thought of it, she wondered what it was that he had seen on the screen when he had swiped her passport, or if he was just in a foul mood and wanted to ruin somebody's day. In all of her years she had never been sent to secondary, and as she had sat there amongst the diverse mix of people she had hoped that she never would be again.

'I have no idea, a random check I guess,' Susan shrugged. 'Maybe he didn't like the look of me.' It wasn't as if no one ever went there from the crew, but they were normally expecting it, like they had a strange passport, or the same name as a criminal. She couldn't help thinking at the time though that they had been looking for something, pulling everything out of her case and checking it thoroughly, even her underwear. She wondered if the others had the same treatment, having a newfound sympathy for them if they did. Anyway, it was what it was, and she had come out unscathed, so she wasn't going to let it ruin anything.

'Anyone for drinks?' The handsome first officer, Ray, who looked equally as lovely out of his uniform, stood in front of them, shrouded in sunlight.

'Oh, I'm okay, I'll get my own,' said Alice. 'Thanks though.'

Susan suspected that she was one of those girls who worried that accepting a drink meant more than that, or that she would be dragged into expensive rounds that she couldn't afford.

'Mojito please,' Susan said, without such a second thought.

'Same here please, Ray,' Emma smouldered next to her.

'Coming up,' he said assertively, walking off in the direction of the bar.

'Do you think he's single?' Emma asked as they all watched him. He was attracting a lot of attention from a group of American girls that stood around, and Susan already found them irritating.

'Does it matter?' she asked her with a straight face, which soon broke into a grin. Emma looked at her in mock horror.

'That would depend,' she said, pulling a thoughtful face.

'On what?' Susan was curious, wondering what made it okay to cheat and what didn't, if other people had the same view on things as her.

'On whether anyone would be likely to get hurt, I guess. On whether his partner works for us too.' The others agreed, that would be crossing an unspoken line.

As they all sipped their drinks they watched him talking to the girls who had by now surrounded him. He looked a little out of his depth as they blatantly flirted, two of them standing either side of him, stroking his arms and flicking their hair around unnecessarily.

'Do you think he needs saving?' Susan spluttered as one of the girls deftly lifted up his t-shirt to reveal a set of abs the likes of which she had never seen, ever. Emma was already up and she followed her quickly. There was a chance that he was actually enjoying the attention really and would rather be left alone, but the forced smile on his face said that he wasn't.

'Do you need a hand with the drinks, Ray?' Susan called, unable to break through them to reach him. A look of relief flashed across his face, and he excused himself clumsily, all the cuter for it.

'Thank you so much, you two. I was drowning there!' He looked genuinely grateful when they sat back down minutes later with their drinks. Susan relished the jealous looks coming from the spurned group, sitting a little closer to him than necessary, just letting them know that they didn't stand a chance.

When they arrived back at the hotel a little before midnight, the effects of the alcohol were being felt by all.

'Come on, Susan, goodnight everyone,' slurred Emma,

grabbing her hand to go to their rooms that were opposite each other on the third floor.

'One sec,' said Susan, breaking away for a moment to hug each of the few that were still huddled in the lobby chatting.

'Room 365,' she whispered in Ray's ear when she reached him last, turning quickly, smiling at her friend and following her to the lift.


Susan undressed quickly, slipping into the cream, pure silk negligee that she had brought with her, just in case, spraying her perfume around the room and on herself. The three knocks on her door were barely audible but she heard them clear as day.... she was expecting them.

# Chapter 18

'Mummy's home for two weeks now,' she said, enthused by the happy looks on their faces in the rear-view mirror. It wasn't like she was away any more days than usual in the month, but her flights just seemed to have been bunched together recently. Jeff had been working late a lot too, and she suspected Lucy could do with a break. Whilst her enabler was always happy to step in and look after the kids, it wasn't her job, she wasn't their mum.

'Right, tell me what's been happening while I was away?'

'Connor asked me out,' Sophia said, blushing.

'Oh, did he now,' Susan said in a light-hearted warning tone, 'I do hope you said no!'

'Of course I did, Mum, I'm too young for a boyfriend.'

Susan was pleased with her answer. 'Good girl, there's plenty of time for boys when you're older.' She might have enjoyed her two lives but it was definitely not what she wanted for her precious daughter. No, she wanted Sophia to have everything that they had now, but with a partner that completed her, so that she didn't have, or want, to find fulfilment elsewhere. She didn't want her to be like her mum, and hoped that she didn't see through her, that she saw Susan Kennedy as her true role model, without a trace of Susan Harrison.

'Daddy's friend Janice came round and she played nerf wars with me.' Lewis's eyes were wide and the grin on his face meant that she couldn't help but smile back at him, but it didn't reflect how she really felt about it. What the hell had that frosty bitch come to her house for? Why was she playing with her son when she couldn't even hold a friendly conversation with his mother? Susan didn't get annoyed easily but that woman was one of her few triggers lately.

'That's nice, darling, I bet you loved that.'

Lewis nodded, still beaming.

'How about we have a family nerf war on Friday night, boys against girls?' She wouldn't be outdone, and Friday nights were their fun nights, when Jeff would come home in a good mood, looking forward to the weekend.

'Yes,' both the children agreed excitedly.

'Lewis was telling me all about his nerf battle with Janice,' Susan said casually as she was getting into bed. Jeff was already under the covers, reading something on his phone.

'Oh, yes.' He had obviously forgotten. 'Yes, Janice had to come here to finish off something, it was that or drag the kids to the office.'

'Was Lucy not around?' Susan asked. She had never known Jeff to invite Janice over, work was always done at the workplace, not here, except for the odd emails maybe.

'Um, yes, she was passing though so it was easier.' He seemed distracted, reading something that was obviously important, so she gave up her line of questioning.

'Oh dear.' He sat up. 'Looks like I'm going to have to go away, seems you're not the only one to leave this month.'

Susan didn't quite understand; go away? Jeff never went away.

'When, where? How come?'

'Paris, on Friday, until Saturday afternoon.' He looked up from his phone apologetically. 'You know I wouldn't go if it was my choice, but one of my biggest clients is insisting on meeting in person, and I can't say no.' He looked pained; travelling for business had worn thin with him many years ago, before they had even met.

'But I promised the kids family nerf wars,' she said, pretending to sulk, although she wasn't wholly pretending, she had actually been looking forward to it. That and the fact she needed to prove that she was much better, and much more fun at it than Jaded Janice. She smirked as her new nickname for her, a private joke with herself.

'We can do that on Saturday,' he said kindly, a look of confused amusement in his eyes, with no inkling as to why his wife had such a sudden urge for the game.

'I know, I could come with you!' Susan hadn't been to Paris for years and could quite fancy a trip to the French capital.

'Really?' Jeff looked at her, unsure. 'I'll be in meetings on both days.'

'Yes, it'll be lovely! I can look around the shops while you're in your meetings, and then you can take me out for a lovely evening afterwards.' She raised her eyebrows and grinned at him; how could he possibly refuse?

'Okay then,' he still sounded unsure, but was agreeing nonetheless, 'sounds like a plan.' He kissed her gently and wrapped his arms around her.

Maybe, Susan thought, a nice weekend away in a beautiful city would make even Jeff exciting and irresistible.

# Chapter 19

Perhaps she was imagining it but Susan was sure there was something wrong with Lucy this morning. She seemed preoccupied, with a constant frown on her face. She needed to ask her to have the children while she went to Paris, but so far there just hadn't been the right moment. It did cross her mind briefly that Luke may have let it slip about their encounter, but no, she didn't seem to be off in that way, not with her anyhow.

*Crash!*

The noise came from the sitting room, followed by a wail of, 'For Christ's sake,' like she could take no more.

Susan tentatively made her way from where she had been making coffee in the kitchen, popping her head slowly around the door. Lucy was knelt down, picking up the pieces of the vase that had just smashed, sobbing.

'Lucy?' Susan was genuinely concerned, she didn't like to see anyone so upset.

Lucy looked up, wiping her tears away quickly.

'I'm so sorry, please take it out of my wages.' She hung her head and carried on picking up the pieces.

'Oh heavens, don't worry about that, I hated the ugly old thing anyway,' Susan retorted, flicking her hand to show that it was forgotten already. She doubted very much that Jeff paid Lucy enough for her to cover the antique with her meagre wages anyway. The big brown vase that now lay in pieces had been given to them by Jeff's parents when they had first moved into the house. Susan had always suspected that they had given it to her just to annoy her, knowing that she would have no choice but to display it, despite it going with nothing else in her carefully and expensively designed interior.

She could hear Lucy's sniffles as she tried to stop her tears, and walked over to her, helping to pick up the pieces.

'I'm sorry,' she said again sadly.

'Lucy, honestly, it's fine.' Susan looked at her but she still hung her head. 'Are you okay?'

'Yes, I'm fine, nothing that will affect my work.' She got up, turning quickly, probably so that Susan couldn't see her tearstained cheeks. 'I'll just go and get the dustpan.'

Susan waited until she came back, perching on the arm of the leather chesterfield. In many ways Lucy reminded her of her own mum, a hard worker, old fashioned, not a taker who thought the world owed her anything, or even that she deserved anything.

'Lucy, do you need some time off?' she asked, finally making eye contact.

'Oh, it's okay, I don't have any leave left anyway. Honestly, I'm fine, it's just my mum's unwell that's all, but I'll get down there at the weekend.' She managed a little smile that Susan was pleased to see, but it didn't hide the worry in her face.

'Oh, please don't worry about leave,' she said kindly.

'If you need some time off, if you need to be with your mum, just go. I'm home for a couple of weeks now and I'm sure the place won't go to complete ruin if I'm left to it!' she joked, trying to lighten the situation. Lucy looked at her, as if she wanted to take her up on the offer but couldn't bring herself to.

'Lucy, please,' she pleaded. 'Honestly, I can manage.' Although she wondered in truth how long she could really stay on top of this house before things started falling apart, hoping deep down that she didn't need too long.

'Okay,' Lucy said finally, 'you're right, I do need some time off, thank you so much.' Her face brightened.

'Right,' Susan said triumphantly, 'now we are getting somewhere, when would be best for you. Today? Tomorrow?'

'My sister's with her today. She's had a heart attack, but they say she's doing okay. Maybe tomorrow until after the weekend?'

'Oh, Lucy, why didn't you say, you poor thing!' Susan couldn't believe that she had even come in today, and respected her now even more than she already had done. 'Now leave that there and get yourself off, go and be with your mum.' She took the dustpan off the dazed Lucy, who stood frozen for a moment, obviously unsure of what to say, or how to take the act of kindness.

'Are you sure?' she asked, still rooted to the spot.

'Go!' commanded Susan in exasperation, pointing to the door.

Lucy threw her arms around her boss, before hurrying through said door.

Susan waved Lucy off from the steps, hoping that everything would be okay when she got wherever down south she needed to be, realising she had never actually asked her. It niggled in the back of her mind that there had been something that she had wanted to ask her, what was it? Paris, of course! Well that had all just put paid to that! She rolled her eyes, realising that she had just sent her only trusted babysitter away at the expense of her own romantic break. Oh well, she resigned herself, it wasn't the end of the world, she wasn't so selfish to think that a night away with Jeff was anywhere near as important as Lucy being with her mum. As she turned and looked around the hall, and through to the living room and kitchen that ran off it, she realised that she had never actually spent a night in the house without Jeff, and she wasn't sure she was going to like it.

# Chapter 20

It felt odd driving to Heathrow in her civvies, not going to work, but when your husband makes the error of all errors and forgets his passport, a wife has to do what she has to do. She glanced at the clock on the dashboard; 11am, she would be back in plenty of time to pick the kids up. It was strange not having the back up of Lucy for everything, but she was coping okay she thought, secretly proud of herself.

She followed the signs to Terminal 5, frustrated by the lane changers who had obviously not been to the airport as often as her, and couldn't work out which lane they needed to be in until they were right underneath the sign that told them.

'I'm just coming.' She called Jeff, making sure that he was waiting for her so that she didn't have to park up. Pulling into the drop off lane she saw him, dressed in his favourite grey blazer, shirt collar open. He waved when he spotted her, jogging quickly over, relief written all over his face. She wound the passenger window down and leant across, holding out the all-important book.

'You can tell you don't come here often,' she teased as he leant in and took it off her, pausing for a moment to catch his breath.

'You're a lifesaver!'

'I know, what would you do without me?' As she smiled at him she saw a woman walking up behind, approaching the car.

'Jeff, we really have to go, they close check-in in five minutes.'

'Coming,' he replied, blowing his puzzled wife a kiss, unable to reach her across the passenger seat to give her a real one.

As he stood up Susan looked at the source of the voice, at first not recognising the smartly dressed woman, with her Louis Vuitton hand luggage.

Jaded Janice looked radiant, hair grown long and so different from the short brown bob that Susan remembered her having the last time she had seen her, albeit a couple of years ago. She'd lost weight too, her navy dress cut on the bias and making her look like a catwalk model. As for her face, the glasses were gone and the makeup was applied beautifully; the ugly duckling that she remembered had become a swan, much to her annoyance.

'Oh, hi, Janice, lovely to see you!' Susan called, waving and smiling through gritted teeth, fighting the urge to add that she hadn't expected to see her here.

'Hello, Mrs Kennedy.' She raised her hand but couldn't even crack a smile. *She could at least* pretend *to like me*, fumed Susan inwardly, watching the pair of them walk away towards the terminal building.


What the hell! Susan drove towards home talking

herself down, trying to stop herself overreacting. No, Jeff hadn't told her that Jaded Janice was going, but she hadn't asked, so he hadn't lied. He hadn't looked even the slightest bit sheepish, so obviously didn't have anything to hide, but even so she wondered if it was really necessary for him to take her to Paris? Well maybe it was, what did she know about the client or the meetings? Perhaps Janice was coming all along?

Susan felt relieved then, that she hadn't had to go with the pair of them, as she wasn't sure how long she could have been nice to her before telling her what she really thought. Anyway, she was quite looking forward to her night on her own with the kids now, with promises of movies and popcorn.

Traffic was fine on the way home, the infamous M25 flowing freely, and she was back by one, two hours free to herself before school time. It was a beautiful day and she sat in the garden for a moment, watching the dogs playing, counting her blessings.

'How are you coping without my aunt?' Luke asked, disturbing her thoughts. She looked up at him; God he was gorgeous, but Susan Harrison wasn't here today. He was grinning as usual, making her feel a little uncomfortable nonetheless.

'Oh, we are fine thank you, Luke, I'll be glad when she gets back though.' There was no harm in being friendly. 'How's your grandmother?'

He was holding a small tool, that he looked down at when she asked.

'Not too good, I don't think,' he said, looking sad, 'but she's in her eighties so I guess it's to be expected.'

'I'm sorry, Luke, if you need to take time off and go down as well, please do.'

'Oh no,' he said with certainty, 'my mum's down there too, I'll get down at the weekend.'

Susan opened her mouth to insist, as she had done with Lucy, but he put his hand up to stop her.

'Honestly I've got too much work on, not just here, and there's loads of us grandchildren, she won't notice if I've been or not.' His one-sided smile was really cute, she thought.

'Well if you're sure, the garden won't go to ruin in a day or two,' she said sincerely.

'It's fine,' he said, not making a move to leave, looking around the garden that he had created. After a short silence, Susan was unusually stuck for anything to say, and was relieved when he spoke. 'If you need me for anything while my aunt's away just ask, I wouldn't mind picking the kids up in the Range Rover!'

'I'm sure you wouldn't,' she laughed at his cheek.

'Right I'd better get on, I want to get those hedges finished today before it gets dark.' He nodded to the hedgerow at the bottom of the garden.

'Don't let me stop you,' Susan said, leaning back in her seat to watch him. It was lovely, she thought, how relaxed she felt without Jeff coming home, not having to play the perfect wife, just being herself in the big house that sat imposingly behind her, for the first time ever.

# Chapter 21

Susan was exhausted, sinking into the sofa between her children. The past two hours had involved running around the house with various plastic guns from Lewis's artillery, firing foam bullets at them both and hiding out. Oh yes, she was *much* more fun than Jaded Janice, she congratulated herself!

The house was in turmoil; she realised that she hadn't really ever appreciated how much Lucy did do, that her children actually created quite a lot of mess that was usually magically cleared up before she had noticed it, on school days at least. Now though, cushions lay scattered across the floor, shoes and school bags dumped in the hall, and the remnants of their pizza dinner were still on the table in the kitchen. Even at the weekends it didn't look like this, Lucy always leaving it spotless on a Friday. The past few days without her were very evident.

'What are we watching then?' she asked her daughter, who had firm possession of the remote control.

'How about this,' she said, stopping on a movie with a group of teens in the picture.

'No,' said Lewis flatly without hesitation. 'That one,' he shrieked as she scrolled straight past an animated film, but that was a definite no from her too.

Susan realised that the decision could take some time yet, and despite committing herself to relaxation in Jeff's absence, she couldn't quite resist her urge to clean up, just a little bit.

'I'll be back in a minute, I'm just going to clear up the kitchen.' Neither of them seemed to notice as she left the room, both engrossed in the endless list of movies, unable to come to any sort of agreement.

The sun was just beginning to set outside, signalling that it was almost certainly time for a glass of champagne. Susan decided that the tidying up could wait just a couple more minutes whilst she opened a fresh bottle and poured herself a glass. She inhaled the bubbles before taking a sip, feeling instantly even more relaxed than she had done already.

As she stood at the sink minutes later she gazed out of the window, surprised to see that Luke was still working at the end of the garden. It was six o'clock, she confirmed with the display on the Rangemaster, surely he needed to be getting home to his new baby soon? Susan was clueless about their finances, not sure if he was paid hourly or otherwise, Jeff took care of all of that, but she was sure that this must be overtime.

'Movie's starting, Mum,' called Sophia from the lounge.

Susan topped up her glass and carried it, and the bottle, through with her. Well she was sure the movie would be a long one after all!

The doorbell rang and the three of them all looked at

each other, no one jumping to answer it. After a moment Susan stood up, feeling the effects of the champagne as she did so, noting the empty bottle on the side. She couldn't work out in her fuzzy head who on earth would be ringing her doorbell at this time. The children had turned back to watch the end of the movie; it was just getting to the good bit and there was no danger of them moving.

Susan opened the door, wishing for a moment that she had a spy hole, like in the hotels, but reasoning that since the property was gated it wasn't really necessary, no one could get in uninvited.

Luke stood on the step looking slightly awkward, shifting his weight from one leg to another.

'I'm really sorry, I was working late, hoping to catch Mr Kennedy when he got home. Will he be back soon, do you know?'

'Sorry, Luke, no, he's away.' Susan felt bad, wondering if he would have gone home hours ago if he'd realised that Jeff wasn't coming back tonight. 'He won't be back until tomorrow evening. Anything that I can help with?'

She doubted very much that she could help with anything that he wanted Jeff for, especially now that the champagne was blurring her judgement. Her cheeks felt warm and she could feel herself being drawn to him, her face unable to compose itself, she felt her eyes widen.

'Oh, no, I just wanted to talk to him about my hours, I could do with an extra day or two to get everything tidied up now that the trees are dropping their leaves. It's okay, it can wait until he gets back anyway.' He didn't move; although nothing more needed to be said Susan had fixed him with her glazed stare and he must have felt the energy coming from her. 'I can show you what

I've been doing today if you like.'

It was almost dark and Susan couldn't see as far down the garden as the hedge that he had been working on, but that didn't matter.... as they only got as far as the summer house.

# Chapter 22

Susan lay in bed the next morning deciding whether it had really happened or if it was just an alcohol-fuelled dream. Deep down she knew that it was real but chose the latter, deciding that there was nothing to be gained by regret, and trusting that Luke would be honourable in his silence. Funnily, the guilt that she'd had last time didn't really come, maybe because Jeff hadn't been here, or maybe because she wasn't panicking so much about being caught out this time. Whatever it was she decided there and then that she wasn't going to think about it anymore.

Despite her thumping head she managed to get herself moving, and was soon flying around the house putting everything back in its place; it wouldn't do for Jeff to come home to this mess. After checking in every cupboard, she finally located the vacuum cleaner, which it seemed no longer lived where it had done the last time she had needed it, pre-Lucy. The children came and went as her chores continued, and she was beginning to feel like Cinderella, still in her dressing gown at midday, wondering how the last three hours had passed so quickly.

She showered, letting the water wash away all traces of Susan Harrison, *she* had to go now as Jeff was due home. She blow-dried her hair, spent time making sure that her makeup was perfect, and chose a smart casual Whistles dress to subtly impress him with when he got home.

An image of Janice came to her mind, and she quickly swapped the dress for something a little more eye-catching, one that she knew Jeff *really* liked. She had competition now, not that she thought for a minute that Jeff would have eyes for anyone else, but how could he think his wife was the most beautiful woman in the world when he looked at an equally, if not more, beautiful one every day at work?

She hadn't thought to check her phone, she had been far too busy all morning, and it wasn't as if Susan Kennedy's social life had her phone ringing off the hook anyway.

He'd said he'd be home about three o'clock, a short meeting in the morning he said, then he'd be flying straight home. Three came and went, and so did four, before she finally located her phone, ready to call him.

*Won't be home until tomorrow morning, client has asked us to stay for dinner and couldn't say no. Sorry xxxxx*

There had been three missed calls and then he had obviously given up and texted her.

*Okay, hope you're enjoying yourself, we miss you xxxx*

It wasn't what she wanted to say, what she wanted to say was that she'd 'just spent all morning being Cinder-effin-rella.' That she'd just spent an hour getting ready for him, no one else was here to appreciate how lovely she looked. That she hoped Jaded Janice was choking on frogs' legs.

Susan stopped herself running away with her angry thoughts, knowing that she was overreacting, but even so, she couldn't help it.

'Kids, get dressed, we're going out.' There was no way she was sitting around the house all dressed up, no way José.

'Where?' called Sophie from her room.

'Bluewater.'

'Yesssss!' came the reply.

Susan doubted her son would be so enthralled about going to the shopping Mecca, he could be bribed though. She climbed the stairs to tell him, suspecting that he had his headphones on and hadn't heard her.

She checked her purse, making doubly sure that the credit card Jeff had given her was in there. They were going to shop with no limits, and then have dinner somewhere really, really nice...on him. He may be in Paris, enjoying dinner at the Eiffel Tower or somewhere equally beautiful, with *her*, but *they* could have a nice time too. She was damned if she was sitting around here all dressed up with nowhere to go, like the mug that she felt.

The best part of three thousand pounds later, and exhausted, they made it home. The clock on the display told her that it was almost 10.30, and she was exhausted. The retail therapy had been just what she'd needed though, and her bad mood had lifted. Sophia was buzzing with her purchases, and even Lewis was happy, with enough Lego to keep him busy until next year; it had been a very successful shopping trip!

She hoped that Jeff wouldn't question the big spend

when the bill came in, but she was ready to blame it on her abandonment issues if he did. He had never questioned one before anyhow, although she didn't recall ever having had such a blowout.

She felt so much better now, it was amazing how money really could buy you happiness, she thought. Now it was like she'd taken a thousand deep breaths, and was ready to face the next day, getting poised for his return all over again.

# Chapter 23

New York immigration had never been the friendliest, but today really was taking the biscuit. The grey-faced, bloated man hadn't even looked at her as he took her passport, but she smiled at him anyway, if only to annoy him if he did.

'Four fingers, right hand,' he barked, and she robotically placed her fingers on the green scanner.

'Camera.' He pointed the small camera at her and she resisted the urge to pull a funny face, pretty sure that it wouldn't go down too well.

He scribbled something on her crew declaration, the one she had filled out earlier to say she had nothing to declare, and thrust it, and her passport, back at her. This was the first time he had looked at her, boring through her with his unblinking eyes. Was that a scowl? It was like a real look of hatred, and she quickly walked off, glad to get away from him. She had a bad feeling though; why hadn't he stamped the form like normal, like every other time, except in Chicago?

Her worst fears were confirmed as she handed it to the

customs officer at the exit and he pointed her towards secondary inspection. *Not again!* What the hell?! Susan couldn't help rolling her eyes, shoulders dropping, but doing as she was told, she had no choice.

'Can you tell the captain I've been pulled in please, hon?' she asked one of the crew who was walking towards her, on their way to freedom.

'Oh no,' the girl said with genuine sympathy, 'hope they don't keep you too long.'

Susan could only manage a shrug; in honesty she was feeling a little upset, and was hoping she wouldn't cry in front of anyone. Once had been bad enough but now it was starting to feel personal.

'We'll hold the bus,' the girl called after her.

Oh seriously?! Susan had been sitting waiting for at least half an hour now, watching the people in front of her be called up one by one to have a stranger go through their personal belongings. She had to admit, some of them did look a bit suspect, but not all, and she was pretty sure that she didn't.

There were three of them searching bags, and she kept everything crossed that when it was her turn the friendly looking young one would call her. Quite frankly the other two scared her. But no, it had to be the worst of the three and she cried silently, as the butch looking woman with close cropped hair, and a face only a mother could love called her over.

'Open your bag, ma'am,' she ordered. Susan lifted her case onto the table and opened it. Butch signalled to the declaration that she was still holding and took it from her, seeming to understand a meaning behind the random letters that he had scribbled on it.

'Anything to declare this time?' she asked, making Susan nervous with her eye contact.

'No,' she said, wondering what she meant by 'this time'; did she know about Chicago?

'Okay, that was your chance to tell me if you did.' She was shaking her head and raising her eyebrows like she thought Susan had lied, starting to unpack her case. She checked *everything*: pockets, toiletries, every nook and cranny. Susan almost had to say something when she was mauling her best underwear, as if she had never seen anything that wasn't from Walmart before, and confirming her earlier suspicions regarding her sexual orientation.

'Okay, you're clean,' she said finally, 'you can pack up now.'

Susan looked at the jumbled pile of clothes and belongings and bit her tongue, struggling to control her anger. The officer took a step back and looked at her; she obviously wasn't going to help, but it seemed she was going to enjoy watching her put everything back, find pleasure in stripping innocent people of their dignity.

'Can I just ask,' Susan started. This was probably a *really* bad idea. You never, ever questioned *them,* unless you want to end up getting the rubber glove treatment! She had started now though so she might as well go on, trying to sound as submissive as possible. 'This is the second time I've been pulled in, is there a reason for it, or is it just random?'

She was looking at her, a sneer on her face.

'Because you got caught before. We don't take kindly to people like you, Miss, you'll be seeing more of us for a while yet.'

'What?' Susan struggled to understand what she was

saying. 'But I've never been stopped with anything before? I've never had anything I shouldn't have!' she protested.

'Well it says here that you have.' Butch was waving the declaration at her, that must have been what the letters meant. 'If you think it's wrong you can contact this department.' She turned and took a leaflet from a pile on the desk behind her, putting it down on the table next to the case. The sneer had gone and Susan suspected, or hoped, that she might possibly believe her. Obviously, she was being confused with somebody else, now it all made sense.

'Thank you,' she said, carefully repacking her bag, putting the leaflet on the top; she would have to sort that out soon if she didn't want to do this every time she came in!

The crew cheered as she got on the bus. She was sure that they hadn't enjoyed having to wait for her, but they knew that she had been having a much worse time than them. She dropped, relieved, into an empty seat, taking her second phone out of her bag. Now that was all over and she could look forward to seeing Tony, she smiled.

*Call me, it's important x*

The message was from Mark.

# Chapter 24

They sat at their table for two, in the window of the restaurant, and watched as the Manhattan skyline slowly passed them by. Tony had surpassed himself this time, bringing her up to The View, the circular restaurant that revolved on the top of The Marriott in Times Square. Susan matched the buildings from the illustration on her cocktail napkin with the ones outside, recognising the gilded folds of the Chrysler Building's roof. She was still awestruck, despite her numerous visits, by the giant structures that surrounded her.

'Hey, Tony,' a broad New York accent interrupted them.

'Hey, Karl, fancy seeing you here.' Tony was up and eagerly shaking the hand of a thirty-something man that she thought she recognised from somewhere. 'Don't tell me you've got a date, man?'

'You better believe it.'

'Awesome, where's the lucky lady?' Tony patted his smiling friend on the arm.

'Like I'd introduce her to you,' he laughed, before noticing Susan sitting down behind him, his face dropping.

'Oh sorry, I didn't mean anything, just that he's such a good-looking guy, you know.'

'Relax,' Tony was amused as his friend tried to stutter his way out of making him look bad, 'she knows what you mean.' He turned and flashed his winning smile at her. She did know, she was under no illusions that someone like Tony was sitting around on his own between her visits.

'Anyway, I'd better go, can't keep the lady waiting. Thanks for the recommendation though, buddy, great place.' Susan wondered how many other *ladies* Tony had brought up there. 'Nice to meet you,' he nodded at her, patting Tony's arm as he walked off.

Tony sat down, shaking his head as he watched his friend walk away.

'That guy, he gets so nervous with women, it's no wonder he can't hold one down.'

'Not like you, huh,' Susan quipped; she did love his confidence but that brief moment when she thought about him with other girls had knocked her from her pedestal slightly. She pulled herself together quickly though, what the hell was she doing? There was absolutely no room for those sorts of emotions in this arrangement! *Get back in the moment, Susan Harrison*, she scolded herself.

Hours later they strolled through Times Square, amongst its bright lights and digital billboards. The city was still wide awake as people made their way home from the theatres on Broadway, or to the next bar. Tony hailed a yellow cab, opening its door for Susan to get in first.

'43rd and Lexington please, driver,' she said, and he nodded his head. She loved the ease of getting around here, the city built like a grid of streets and avenues, everything found by its position between them.

Tony put his arm around her and pulled her towards him. He smelt so good, even better than usual, she thought, impatient to get him back to the hotel. Of course, he had already been to her room when she had arrived, the routine never changed, nor did she want it to.

As Tony paid the driver five minutes later, Susan went on ahead to her room, surprised when she got there to hear the sound of her phone ringing. Mark, again, what on earth could be so important? She definitely wasn't going to speak to him now, but she was beginning to think that maybe she should call him back soon, perhaps it really was something important.

The sound of the door opening snapped her out of her wondering, and she turned the phone off; the last thing she wanted was Mark to be disturbing her when she was with Tony!

'Susan, I'm so glad you called me back, I've been trying to get hold of you.' Mark sounded so relieved, she hoped he'd calm down in a minute though as it wasn't very attractive. She liked her companions to be calm and confident, not needy and flustered.

'Mark, I don't use this phone at home,' she said flatly. She had put him on speaker as she got ready for work. Tony had left a couple of hours ago, and now she was just putting the finishing touches to her makeup, hoping that it wouldn't take too long to clear up whatever this was with Mark.

'I know, but I was just hoping you might turn it on.' He was still too excitable. 'Anyway, it might be nothing, but, my wife found out about us.'

'*What?*' Susan stopped what she was doing, mascara wand held aloft. 'How the hell, Mark?' She was furious, how could he have let it happen? She took a deep breath; his wife was in San Diego, it wasn't that bad, exhale.

'She had someone follow me last time I came to San Francisco.' He was slowing down now, as if uncertain how to go on.

'Right,' Susan said slowly, 'and how much does she know?'

'Everything.'

What the hell did that mean? What was *everything*?

'Like your name,' he said. Susan felt her stomach lurch. 'And the airline you work for.' Now she felt sick.

'Mark, I really hope this is just a bad joke.'

'I'm so sorry, I didn't realise she would go this mad. We haven't been right for years, but she wants to take everything in the divorce and now she's got proof I was cheating on her. They've even got this phone number from my phone records, and know that you bought it in Target on whatever date it was.'

Susan looked at the innocent phone. She remembered signing her name the day that she bought it, but never could have foreseen that it would come back and haunt her like this. She was speechless.

'They got photos of us together on the ferry, too.'

He'd obviously got everything out that he needed to and the line was silent for a moment. She tried to process what he was telling her, whether it was likely to threaten Susan Kennedy. She hoped that the different surnames would be enough for the trail to end with her job, that the woman would be happy enough with the evidence against Mark, and not need revenge on her too.

'Mark,' she said slowly, 'is she likely to cause any trouble for me?' Maybe she was being selfish, but quite frankly Mark's divorce was not her problem. Or it shouldn't have been.

'I don't know, it's just...' he stalled.

'Just what?'

'She works for Customs.'


Susan was completely distracted as she walked through the lobby, her mind whirring, going around in circles. What the hell was she capable of? Of course it must have been her that had fixed her records and got her pulled in. She hoped that the email that she had just sent would be enough to get her record cleared.

She would have to shake it off though, hope that it would end there, what else could she do? Seeing the other crew forced her back into the moment, and as they left through the revolving door she turned back to see Tony watching her; she smiled at him, and then at the man he was standing with, in his doorman's uniform, the man from last night who clearly recognised her as he grinned knowingly.

# Chapter 25

'How is your mum, Lucy?'

'Oh, she's doing great, thanks, she's a tough old bird.'

Susan had been so relieved to get Lucy back after ten long days away, returning from New York to an immaculate house. It wasn't that she hadn't coped without her, but there had been no time for the gym or pampering herself when she had to take care of the domestic things too. It had made her realise though, how much she had taken for granted in her enchanted life, and appreciate it all the more so.

'Lucy, I've been meaning to ask you something.' She stopped to make sure she had her attention.

'I'm listening,' Lucy confirmed, not looking up from the floor that she was meticulously cleaning.

'It's just that we are off on holiday at the end of the month, and I was wondering if you would be able to come and stay here, look after the house and the dogs?' She had left it late to ask her, had meant to do it before she went away, but she already knew the answer.

'Of course, let me know the dates.' She was looking up

now, straight-faced but her eyes were smiling. Susan had known she would jump at the chance to be the lady of the house, and now she could go on their holiday without any concerns.

'Lucy, you're a superstar, thank you so much. I will make sure Jeff makes it worth your while financially.'

'That's very kind of you, thank you.'

'Right I'm off to the gym, see you later,' Susan called as she left, 'and thanks again.'

'You're welcome,' Lucy called after her, sounding happy at the prospect of her upcoming job and its extra payment.

The class was a killer, and as they all took the two minutes the instructor was giving them to catch their breath, Susan sat on her step, wiping the sweat off her with her towel.

'Susan, I haven't had a chance to thank you for your recommendation.' Laura, the new girl, was sitting on her mat next to her, in as much of a sweaty mess as she was. Susan had no idea what she was talking about, feeling like her brain was a wobbling jelly right now.

'The gardener,' Laura grinned. 'Luke.'

Of course, Luke, but why was she looking at her like that when she said his name, all wide-eyed?

'Oh yeah, how's he working out?' she asked casually.

'Oh really, *really* well thanks,' Laura said slowly, still looking at Susan with that look that she thought she should be able to read, but couldn't.

'Right, ladies, back to work,' called the instructor. Susan lifted her tired body up, glancing sideways at Laura, who was biting her bottom lip, failing to hide the devilish look on her face.

Susan was gobsmacked, finding herself looking at Laura multiple times during the rest of the class. Laura just kept grinning back, obviously amused by her shocked look.

'You never mentioned how hot he was,' she finally said when they had a chance to talk as the session finished and the music stopped, 'and soooo good in the garden too.'

'Laura, are you trying to tell me something?' Susan said quietly, not sure whether her imagination was running away with itself. She had only met this girl a couple of times, and didn't really know anything about her after all. Was she referring to his skills with a hedge trimmer or something else? Did she have a summerhouse too?! Perhaps she wasn't the only one who had fallen for his charms?!

'No,' she said, too easily, too brightly, her eyes saying different, 'anyway thanks again, he's *amazing*. Got to dash, hair appointment.' She picked up her bag and walked off quickly. Susan was speechless, her mouth agape as she watched her walk away.

As Susan drove home she thought over what had happened. She couldn't understand why she was feeling off kilter, why the thought of Luke with Laura bothered her, made her jealous even. She really had thought that Luke was only attracted to her because she was something special, not that he was available to anyone who was on offer. Laura was attractive, fair enough, but she wasn't all that!

It made her feel, well, she wasn't sure how it made her feel. A little less special? A bit used maybe? She looked in the rear-view mirror at her reflection; was she losing her looks? Was she not as irresistible as she thought that she was? Well that couldn't be the case, she had never been turned down by a man yet, but was that just because they were all just after one thing?

She had always thought that if she had wanted any of them for more than an arrangement that they would have received her gratefully. Now though, she wondered if she was deluded and that perhaps they were using her as much as she was using them. What with Tony's friend hinting that he was a bit of a Lothario, and now Luke, she could feel her confidence faltering, digging deep to set it back up high.

By the time she got home she had had a strong word with herself. Luke was just taking what was offered, and the others were still the exciting gorgeous men that they had been, nothing had changed. Then there was Jeff, and she knew that he adored her, so why was she letting something that really didn't matter bother her when she had everything? Susan Harrison didn't need any more from any of them than the 'in the moment' excitement that they gave her, and whether they got that elsewhere as well was neither here nor there, as long as she didn't know about it.

As she drove up her driveway Luke was walking past, giving her a friendly wave. She waved back, smiling, making sure that he was watching her, reading her. Her moment of insecurity had passed, she was better than that, and better than Laura.

# Chapter 26

The kids were at school, Jeff was at work, and no one else should have been around, only Susan had forgotten about Lucy, as she was almost invisible in her constant presence.

'*Luke!*'

The shout was so unexpected that neither of them stopped in their moments of gratification, the summer house windows steamed up as they had been regularly these past two weeks. Susan couldn't have explained it, not even to herself, but since the conversation with Laura at the gym she had had this insatiable need to be irresistible to Luke, and here they were.

'*Luke!*'

There it was again. The chances now that it was just a fox screaming, or the sound of another wild animal in the fields were almost zero, and as they both fell silent it was clear that the strangled voice they both knew belonged to Lucy, and she needed her nephew, right now.

'I'm so sorry.' Luke kissed her hungrily, pulling himself up and reaching for his trousers. Susan shook her head to say 'don't worry'; she knew that Lucy would not be calling like that unless there was an emergency, and she hoped that it wasn't what she thought that it was.

She let five minutes pass before she emerged, ducking quickly behind the wooden building so that she could make it look as if she hadn't come from the same direction that he had, just in case anyone was watching. She walked slowly, and casually, back up to the house, picking a few flowers from the borders to justify her entrance from the garden.

When she reached the pool, Lucy was in Luke's strong arms, head buried in his beautiful chest, sobbing.

'Lucy?'

Luke shook his head, and Susan knew in that moment that her mum hadn't made the great recovery that everyone had hoped for. She felt the sinking feeling in her stomach, the overwhelming sympathy for the lovely woman who asked nothing from anyone making her own heart ache.

'I'm so sorry.' It was all that she could say, and she stood silently on the edge of their grief until someone was able to speak.

'We need to go, is that okay?' Luke asked, no explanation needed.

Susan nodded, tears pricking her eyes.

'Please, be where you need to be, I'm so sorry.'

Luke looked at her gratefully, turning and leading his broken aunt, who was crying uncontrollably now, to her car. He put her gently into the passenger seat and climbed in the driver's side to take her away. Susan stood at the front of the house; there was nothing to say, she had never seen raw grief before and she had no idea how she should react to it. In that moment she realised how lucky she had been never to lose anyone so close to her, although she wondered if perhaps she had never been that close to anyone to grieve for them like this, even her own mother.

She waved them off soberly, knowing that it was the only right thing to do, to let them both go without a second thought. Of course, she would also make sure that Jeff paid them, because that was the nice and kind boss that she was, and she would keep on top of things here. As she stood on the step almost enjoying her moment of martyrdom she remembered the chaos of just two weeks ago, and let out a small involuntary groan. Oh well, it couldn't be helped, and at least she knew where the cleaning products were now!

Susan turned to walk back into the house; she needed a vase to put these flowers in. She felt sad, but grateful at the same time, that it wasn't her that was sobbing, grateful that life was still good for her at this moment. She just hoped that Lucy would be back in time for their trip to Dubai in twelve days!

# Chapter 27

'Thank you so much, Lucy, but honestly, if you need more time then please just say, I can arrange kennels for the dogs. Hopefully we will see you then.'

Susan hung up the phone, relieved that Lucy would be back in just a few more days. Of course, she had had to offer her more time, how could she not, but deep down she had kept everything crossed that she wouldn't need it. She looked around the kitchen, still messy from breakfast, and rolled her eyes. Lucy couldn't get back soon enough for her.

Jeff had made her cancel her flight this week, he couldn't manage the children's school and work on his own, he said, more like he didn't want to, she suspected. Perhaps if she had had a little break she wouldn't be resenting cleaning up after the three of them so much right now. She mustn't complain though, in five days they would be off to Dubai, and she would be waited on hand and foot.

'Back to work, Cinders,' she muttered under her breath as she began to sweep the expanse of floor, beginning to lose her love of the large house, wishing sometimes lately that it was just a fraction smaller!

An hour later she had finally made her way upstairs, making the children's beds whilst wondering at what age they should really be doing this for themselves. She sat down on Sophia's bed for a moment and took in the things around her, the little trinkets and makeup on her dressing table, the school books scattered across her floor, ballet pumps hanging from the rail at the bottom of her bed. She hoped that her daughter realised how much she loved her, hoped that she was doing a better job of showing it than her own mum had. It wasn't that her mum had been bad, just a little detached with her own problems, not really present in her mind when Susan had needed her advice and guidance. She knew she wasn't a perfect wife sometimes, but she tried her hardest to be a perfect mother, and she thought she did a pretty good job.

Moving on to her own room she made the oversized bed, placing the numerous cushions back exactly where she liked them, hearing in her mind Jeff's repeated protests that they were pointless. A quick look at her watch told her that it was nearly one o'clock and she thought for a moment of how to make the best use of her remaining time before the school run. *I know*, she thought, *I'll make a start on packing*. Usually something that she left until the last minute, she realised that she would need to be a little more prepared for this trip, with four of them to think about. Sure, Jeff would probably be happy to do his own, but that would mean his usual carefree attitude to his appearance, and that wasn't what she had in mind for this holiday.

Walking into the wardrobe she surveyed the two rails

from which his few garments hung; well, few in comparison to her eight rails that bowed with the weight they bore, and she took out the shirts that she would allow him to bring. A shopping trip would definitely be needed before they went, maybe Sophia would come with her after Jeff got home this evening, to save them dragging Lewis around.

She sighed at the sight of the grey blazer jacket that he insisted on wearing everywhere. It wasn't that she disliked it, in fact it rather suited him, it was just that every memory she had of them going anywhere he seemed to be wearing it. She brushed some specks from the collar and held it up, eyeing it critically, knowing that he would definitely want to wear it to the airport at least. For a moment she considered taking it to the charity shop, but she doubted they would be overwhelmed by the well-worn offering either, and she couldn't bear to hurt Jeff's feelings for the sake of being mean. Perhaps a trip to the dry cleaners could freshen it up a little, she thought, emptying the pockets.

As Susan placed the small handful of receipts and pocket fluff on top of the shoe cabinet that ran around the room, something caught her eye. She unfolded the piece of paper, confirming that the little tree she had seen was indeed the symbol for her favourite designer handbag shop. The two-thousand-euro amount that it was for showed that he had bought something very nice there too. In fact, as she scrutinised it further, it was the specific bag she had been coveting for weeks, the latest must-have, and the date showed that he had bought it when he was in Paris recently.

She looked around the wardrobe, hoping to see the

bag, to find her gift that he had obviously bought her. It was still weeks until Christmas, and she wasn't sure that she could wait that long! It couldn't be that hard to find, she told herself, she had had bags from there before and the oversized, overstated packaging was a gift in itself. She looked in every drawer and cupboard, under the bed and behind it, but nothing was to be found, and the house was too big to search every room. Exasperated, and noticing the time, she gave up. She would just have to wait until he was ready to give it to her, she resigned herself, and Susan hated waiting!

# Chapter 28

It was so lovely to fly with another airline, in a business class seat, being looked after like a proper passenger. For a fraction of the price she could have flown with Osprey on standby, but firstly they may not have got on, and secondly, they may not have been be upgraded. Flying in economy would not have been a good start for their holiday, especially when your husband was loaded and there was no need to turn right, unless she was working of course.

The flight attendant handed her a glass of champagne, and Susan resisted the urge to tell her to leave the bottle, she would definitely be getting her money's worth today. Jeff handed her his grey jacket, which did look marginally better for being cleaned she thought, not that he had even noticed.

She looked behind her and grinned at her children, who were excited by the way their seats turned into beds. She had made sure to tell them that they were very lucky to travel like this, and not to think that it was normal for most people. Their excitement pleased her, showing that they didn't take it for granted, although it was probably because they didn't get to have holidays as often as they probably should. She would definitely have to start being more proactive with booking them.

As she turned back around Jeff took hold of her hand and squeezed it; he was smiling at her and looking the most relaxed and contented that she had seen him in a very long time. It wasn't that he ever seemed stressed really, more tired from the ever longer days that work was demanding of him, sometimes not getting home until past eight o'clock and having to leave again before seven in the morning. She studied his face and felt a warmth that made her own face mirror his, and she squeezed his hand back; the Kennedys were going to have a wonderful holiday.

The hotel was everything that she had thought it would be, and the delighted squeals of the children running around their suite confirmed that they were just as impressed. The huge orange-hued building hadn't looked real as they had driven up to it, magnificent and ornate, with its huge wings stretching out either side of its central arch. They had been escorted by the concierge through the expansive lobby with its jaw dropping flower displays, checking in downstairs in the club level reception. Here they were now in their two-bedroom suite that looked out over the Palm, the man-made landmark, and its white sand beaches famous around the world.

'Dad, what are you wearing?' Sophia cried, Lewis giggling by her side. Susan turned to see Jeff, who she had thought was just using the bathroom, standing proudly in a short-sleeved shirt that was covered in bright green palm trees.

'What the heck is that?' she asked, horrified. She had never seen it before, and certainly hadn't packed it.

'Do you like it?' he asked, lifting his eyebrows up and down and pulling funny poses that had their son almost in tears he was laughing so much.

Susan just shook her head slowly, no, she really didn't like it. She looked to her daughter for support; surely Sophia would be on her side with this?

'Sophia, tell your father that he can't wear that out!'

Sophia though was smiling, maybe not quite as amused as her brother, but not as horrified as she would have been had they been at home.

'It's my holiday shirt, and I like it, I don't care what you think!' Jeff obviously didn't give a hoot about what his wife thought, which irked her even more. 'Right, get your swimming stuff on, we are going to the pool!' he announced.

Susan stood speechless, the words that she wanted to say trapped in her head. The three of them scattered to find their costumes, leaving her to come to terms with what had just happened. She struggled with the part of her that just wanted him to fit into her ideals, and the mother that loved that he was making their children laugh. She would have to let it go, she concluded quickly, it was his holiday too, and if he wanted to wear that awful shirt then she would have to accept it, whether she liked it or not. The fact that there was absolutely no way that she could be attracted to a man that thought so little about his appearance was extremely unfortunate.

# Chapter 29

Lucy stepped out of the shower feeling invigorated. She had had no idea that a shower could do so many things, make you feel so good with its pulsating jets and steam functions. She thought of her own basic one at home, the one that sat over her bathtub and just about managed to rinse the shampoo from her hair, but what else could she expect from a value brand?

She dried herself off with the new white Egyptian cotton bath towel. Mrs Kennedy always requested that they were replaced every six months with brand new ones. Lucy had always thought that it was a little bit spoiled, but was grateful nonetheless to take the old ones home, nothing wrong with them after all. Now though, now that she was living this life for a short while, she had to agree that new ones did feel that much fluffier and more luxurious.

Pumping the expensive body cream into her hand she smoothed it over every inch of her body, breathing in the exotic aroma, loving the way that it felt on her skin. She had never seen the brand on the shelves at Asda, and she was pretty sure that it would have a huge price tag wherever it was stocked.

As she stood in the wardrobe moments later, she surveyed the rails of designer clothes, choosing a blue woollen wrap dress for today, admiring how it made her slim figure look curvy in the long mirror. It was a shame that the endless rows of shoes were just a little big for her, but it didn't stop her from trying on a few pairs just to see what they looked like with the outfit, even if she couldn't walk in them.

Lastly, she sat at the dressing table and opened the drawer of makeup, applying the brands to her face that she could never have justified buying. She had always wanted to believe that it didn't really matter what brand your makeup was, that the cheap ones were just as good, but she had discovered yesterday that some of these little pots and palettes could perform small miracles. She had always known that she was no beauty but she had to admit that the person who was looking back at her now from the mirror was a much, much more attractive version of herself.

Pleased with her work she breezed down the stairs, slipping on her shoes, the only thing about her right now that was her own, picked up the keys from the console table and walked out to *her* car. As she drove the Range Rover out of the gates she felt euphoric. This was the life she was meant to be leading, it was her that deserved this car, these clothes, not the woman who blatantly cheated on her husband with her own nephew. Did they both think that she was stupid when they snuck off to the summer house? Did they not see her in the window?

Lucy shook her head, momentarily catching herself, shocked at the malice in her own thoughts. She hadn't felt herself since her mum had died, probably because of the difficulty sleeping; yes that was it, once she got a good night's sleep she would be okay, back to her old self she was sure. Yes, it did upset her the way that James were carrying on, but as for deserving her life, and the other troubling thoughts she'd been having, those weren't like her, and they made her uneasy.

She drove the car towards M&S. She knew she was doing wrong, that she was pretending to be someone else, but what harm could it do, to live this life just for a few days? Anyway, Mrs Kennedy wouldn't mind her borrowing the car, she knew that, but perhaps the clothes were a little too much.

She shook her head again, swinging between the reality and the justification. Well she was here now, wearing these clothes, driving this car, so she may as well follow it through and enjoy it. Parking the car, she stepped out and smoothed down her dress. She tried to ignore her cheap shoes, holding her head high as she joined the rest of the Mrs Kennedys in the aisles, gliding along with them, worthy.


'Lucy Skinner, is that you?' Lucy turned to see a vaguely familiar face smiling back at her and she quickly put the ready meal for one that she had just decided on back on the shelf. 'It's me, Kate.' Lucy still couldn't quite place her. 'Kate James, from school!'

'Oh, of course!' Suddenly the penny dropped and Lucy could see that the woman who was standing in front of her, carrying her designer handbag, with her perfectly blow-dried blonde hair, was the same Kate James that she had been in awe of at school. The Kate James who got dropped off every day in her mum's Mercedes, who always looked so perfect, that every boy wanted to go out with. Lucy had just been average, plain even, and her mum didn't own a car, but Kate had always been kind to her, although she couldn't say they had ever been friends. The old feelings of inferiority bubbled up to the surface, and she hoped they didn't show on her face. 'How lovely to see you, Kate, you look really well,' she stammered.

'And so do you!' Kate was wide-eyed, looking her up and down. 'Lucy, you look so lovely.'

Lucy felt herself blush. Kate had always been quick with the compliments though, always said nice things to people, it was just the way that she was. As she looked down she suddenly noticed her dress and remembered that, actually, today she did look good, today of all days perhaps she really did mean it! She tucked her feet underneath her trolley, as only the shoes would give her away.

'Thank you, Kate,' she smiled, relaxing. 'How are you?'

It was amazing how clothes and makeup had given her the confidence to talk to Kate on such an equal level. They stood in the aisle for at least a quarter of an hour as Kate told her about her husband and her job, and Lucy told her about hers. With little else to draw on she found herself back in her fantasy of being Mrs Kennedy, only her children were grown up and Jeff was only a little older than her. She sensed Kate's envy, she could feel that she was lonely in her own marriage, without any children, and it felt good to be the one that was envied. She fought the urge to tell her the truth, to make her feel better, but no, for today at least she was the one with everything, why shouldn't she have a taste of being the one who people wanted to be for the first time in her life?

* * *

Back at the house Lucy looked in horror at the food on the kitchen island, receipt in her hand. She wondered if it was the done thing to take food back. She hadn't been able to stop herself showing off, putting things in her trolley for her imaginary meals with Jeff, with Kate following her around like a long-lost best friend. Now as she looked at the Beef Wellingtons and smoked salmon, the coffee beans and herbal tea bags, she berated herself for spending almost half of her week's salary on things that she didn't even really like, and all because she had started this whole lie. Kate hadn't left her side, even walking her to her car, so in awe was she of how she had done so well for herself, so happy for her, so Lucy hadn't had a chance to put it back, or dump it on a shelf. If only she knew the truth.

She pulled the dress over her head, throwing it angrily on the floor and stood in her underwear, fists clenched by her side. The dogs, that had been quietly waiting to be fed, looked at her with confused, cute faces that made her smile for a second. Maybe they would like Beef Wellington for dinner?

# Chapter 30

Well, once he had taken the ridiculous shirt off and put it in the locker things had turned out wonderfully. The children had dragged them straight to the water park of course, although maybe dragged wasn't the right word, they had hailed one of the complimentary buggies that drove them straight there, along the beach. There was no need to queue and buy tickets, like the rest of the public, not when you were staying in the hotel.

The waterpark was as over-the-top as the hotel was, and the morning had passed quickly as they had gone from one ride to another, their ages irrelevant as they each carried their inflatables up the stairs for the next one. She couldn't remember the last time they had all had this much fun together, *really* enjoyed each other's company like they were now.

Having finally insisted on a break, she watched from her sun lounger as the three of them walked back over from the ice cream stand. They were all laughing at something, and she loved to see the enjoyment on their faces. She couldn't have wished for a more perfect family at that moment.

'Here, Mum.' Lewis handed her a tub of ice cream and she sat up to take it, adjusting her bikini to make sure that it stayed in place.

'Thank you, darling, I think Mum's going to get fat on this holiday,' she grinned, remembering the extravagant buffet they had had only a few hours before.

'I'll have that then.' Jeff playfully took it off her. 'I can't go home with a fat wife!'

The children laughed as Susan tried to grab it back off him, wondering if she actually wanted it now when he finally returned it. She had absolutely no intention of getting fat, ever, but it had never occurred to her that Jeff would love her any less if she did. She watched her husband as they all sat in silence eating, and wondered for a moment if he really meant anything by what he had just said, if he cared about her looks as much as she cared about his? Did he even know that she cared as much as she did, or had she kept it hidden as well as she thought she had?

'Right, who's for the lazy river?' Jeff stood up, empty tub in his hand, and stretched. 'I could do with floating around for a while.'

Susan looked at him; he was definitely looking fitter now, the excess weight around his middle almost gone, and she unquestionably found him more attractive again, but she didn't want him to get too confident, the balance had to be right. He must always be grateful to have her, or one day he might think he could do better, and then where would she be?

'Can you tie me up please, darling?' She applied a quick slick of lip gloss, and ran her fingers through her hair. Standing up slowly, now that she had his attention, she made sure that he was watching her as she smoothed her toned stomach, and stretched out her lean arms and legs. She turned around and moved her hair out of the way so that he could tie the straps of her small but expensive bikini, knowing that he was admiring her, balance restored.

Susan made sure that she walked in front as they made their way to the lockers by the entrance to the lazy river. She knew she was getting admiring glances from the men, and she didn't care about the less favourable ones she was getting from the women. They probably just wished they too could dress the same as her, instead of hiding themselves beneath the long sleeves and trousers that their religion dictated they wear.

'I'll catch you up,' Jeff called, and she turned to see him with his phone to his ear. 'Work,' he mouthed, and she rolled her eyes. This was his first call, in fairness, and she had expected no less, knowing that he would need to be somewhat available.

Susan floated around in her ring, eyes closed behind her sunglasses, leaning back and enjoying the warmth of the sun on her body. She hadn't seen the children for a while; the river seemed to have endless options for you to take, and they were favouring the more exciting, and less relaxing routes. She marvelled at how things had changed since the last time they had a holiday together, at how she could just let them go off and not worry. She was confident that their swimming lessons had paid off now, and also the presence of a lifeguard at least every twenty metres was a huge reassurance. She didn't know if Jeff was still on his call, or trying to find them, but she was sure she would bump into him eventually. Opening her eyes momentarily she saw a handsome lifeguard staring down at her, smiling broadly.

'How are you, madam?' he asked.

'Very well thank you,' she said, with a coy smile, and without sitting up. She let his eyes wander over her, not the slightest bit uneasy with his stares, enjoying them, as she moved slowly past.

'Come back soon,' he called as she drifted away. She knew nothing would or could happen here, but she closed her eyes and imagined anyway, there was no harm in that.


'Susan.' Jeff's voice brought her back into the moment, and she opened her eyes. She was back in the entrance to the river, and he was standing holding on to her ring to stop her floating away again. He looked serious. 'I have to go back to the room for a bit, have to make a call.'

'Really?' She sat up and looked at him.

'I know.' He looked as unhappy about it as she did. 'Hopefully it won't take long but one of my biggest clients needs to speak to me urgently, and there's no one else that can deal with it.'

'Okay, well we'll stay around here, come and find us when you get back.'

'Mum, Dad!' They both looked to see an excited Sophia and Lewis paddling back into the river with their inflatables, waving furiously, and they waved back at them.

'I won't be long, hopefully.' He kissed her quickly and headed off to get a buggy back to the hotel.

For a moment Susan felt disappointed that her family holiday was being interrupted by work, but then that was what being married to someone so successful entailed, she guessed, shrugging off her annoyance. She pushed herself off and felt the current take her, heading back in the direction of her admirer, ready for another dose of appreciation to feed her soul.

# Chapter 31

*What had she done!* Lucy paced up and down the hall, stopping for a moment to check herself in the mirror. The buzzer sounded, and she walked over and pressed the button to open the gates, hearing the sound of the car pulling up the driveway.

Why hadn't she just changed the last digit when she had given Kate her number? Well she hadn't really expected her to ring, hadn't known that she *really* meant it when she had suggested 'popping over one day'. Now, just three days later, and here she was, driving up to her imaginary life, and the tangled web of lies was about to get a whole lot more tangled.

Not only that, nooooo, that would have been bad enough, but Kate had just messaged this morning to say that she was bringing Natasha Thomas with her too, and 'wasn't it lovely that they were all getting together again!' Lucy wailed inwardly, no it wasn't bloody lovely! Natasha Thomas had been a complete stuck-up bitch at school, and the last person she wanted in her imaginary life right now.

She took a deep breath as she opened the door, reminding herself that to them this was all real, that they didn't know the truth. She fixed a smile on her face and welcomed them into her home, surprised at how she enjoyed the look of envy on their faces, slipping rather too easily into the role of Mrs Kennedy. She relished showing them around, lapping up their compliments, enjoying the confidence that money gives you.

'Lucy, you are so lucky, you have everything I dream of having,' Natasha had sighed as she sipped her herbal tea. Of course, she was comparing all of this to her comfortable four-bed detached, and had she only known Lucy lived in a flat she wouldn't be saying that, in fact she probably wouldn't be giving her the time of day.

'I know I am,' Lucy had said humbly.

As she said goodbye a couple of hours later she knew that they couldn't come back here again, she would have to give up all of this soon. She had actually enjoyed their afternoon together, still surprised at how differently people treated you when they thought you were rich, knowing that if they only knew the truth they wouldn't have been so keen to meet up again.

The lies and tales had come easily, her imaginary life was almost real in her mind now, and she was going to miss it. She had always been quite content with what she had, but now she wondered if she could be again, or would she always want more now that she had had a taste of all of this? Anyway, the Kennedys would be back in just a couple of days, and she would just have to get on with it; there was no point in moping about what she couldn't have, her practical voice scolded her.

Lucy didn't really drink, but she only had two more nights to be Mrs Kennedy and so she clumsily opened a bottle of champagne and poured herself a glass. The bubbles went up her nose and she recoiled slightly before taking a sip, wondering what it was about the stuff that her boss loved so much. She felt the effects almost instantly, a warmth in her cheeks, and a happy feeling that made her want more.

She carried the bottle upstairs and ran herself a bubble bath, pouring another glass to enjoy whilst she was in it. She doubted that she could finish the bottle but she was happy to try nonetheless.

When she had dried herself off and applied her creams she went one step further than she had done before, choosing herself a silk nightdress from the dresser and climbing into the fine Egyptian cotton sheets of the Kennedys' bed. She would sleep here and not in the guest room as she had done the previous nights; if she was going to have this life for just two more days then she was going to have it completely. She placed a pillow next to her, imagining that it was her husband, something she had never managed to find.

Lucy closed her eyes and squeezed the imaginary man, suddenly feeling stupid. It was one thing pretending to have this life but perhaps she was going too far now? She sat up and took the glass from the side of the bed, gulping down its contents.

# Chapter 32

'Seriously?' Susan looked at Jeff in disbelief as he got up from the table with the phone stuck to his ear. It was their last night, the children had gone to the kids' club, and they were about to order dinner in what was possibly the most beautiful restaurant she had ever been in. A huge manta-ray swam past, smiling it seemed, one of a thousand sea creatures in the huge tank that made up the restaurant walls. What irritated her even more was that he didn't even look sorry, so common had these interruptions become on their holiday.

She signalled for a waiter, ordering a bottle of champagne to keep her company whilst she waited for him. She knew that Jeff was hoping for a romantic end to their evening, so he had best make an effort to be attentive when he came back, or she might just get a headache, she thought sourly.

'Can you please turn your phone off now,' she pleaded when he returned, half a bottle of champagne later.

'I guess so, it's nearly five o'clock,' he said hesitantly, looking at his watch.

'Can't Janice just take a message for you?'

'Yes, yes, you're right, sorry.' He switched the phone off and put it face down on the table. 'You look beautiful tonight, my love,' he said, looking at her as if for the first time, despite them having come down from the room together. Obviously, he couldn't switch off from work within office hours, she realised reluctantly.

'Thank you,' she accepted his compliment, knowing that she had put in an extra effort this evening, even down to the diamonds that hung from her ears. 'You don't look so bad yourself.'

It was true though, the sun had tanned Jeff's skin and it suited him, taking years away. When he hadn't been on the phone he had been great company this holiday, and helped by the setting and atmosphere here she had really rediscovered her old feelings for him. She hadn't even minded when he had worn that awful shirt again, remembering that it was his sense of humour that she had once found so attractive.

The manta-ray swam back past, still with the smile that was probably not even its mouth almost pressed up against the glass. A shoal of small silver fish followed it, as a thousand eyes turned, it seemed, to look at them.

'Looks like we have company for dinner,' laughed Jeff. 'I guess the seafood is a no go?'

'Looks like it,' agreed Susan, amused, knowing exactly what he meant. She didn't think it would be appropriate to eat seafood whilst being watched by this lot either!


Susan sighed as she packed the suitcases the next morning. She had sent Jeff and the children off to the aquarium for one last visit whilst she sorted things out, and was actually enjoying the peace and quiet. The holiday had been lovely, everything she had hoped that it would be, and last night had turned out to be truly magical. She had enjoyed being Susan Kennedy, on holiday with her family, and she couldn't help being a little sad to go home, where her world was becoming a little tainted. Luke would be waiting for her she was sure, and she doubted that she would be able to resist him. She disliked herself for her lack of willpower, that she couldn't, even now, feeling as happy with Jeff as she was, commit herself to monogamy and find happiness in a simple life. It was just too easy to take the excitement, and she guessed that made her selfish, maybe she should try a bit harder.

Back in her own clothes, Lucy walked from room to room making sure that everything was perfect for the Kennedys' return, that no signs of her double life had been left. The bed was changed, the bathroom cleaned, and everything put back in the drawers and cupboards from which they had come. She stood in the mirror for a moment and looked at her reflection, the old trousers and jumper looking even more tired now than they had done a week ago, before she started to wear the designer clothes.

She looked at the bed in which she had slept these past two nights, grateful to it for giving her two wonderful nights of sleep, although maybe the champagne had helped. She could feel her old self coming back now, the crazy, double-life-living, dark-thought-having Lucy's voice not quite so loud anymore. Now the contented, calm Lucy's voice was the loudest, and she was relieved. She had had a week with the other one and she had exhausted her. She was thankful that she was going, just in time for the

Kennedys to return and things to go back to normal.

As she glanced out of the window she saw her nephew at the bottom of the garden, and realised that the Kennedys' return would probably mean more of the steamed-up windows in the summer house. The calmness Lucy had felt began to subside. The other voice was back, and it was angry. *She* didn't deserve this life, Lucy did!

# Chapter 33

You just couldn't tell some people.

'No, madam, your baby cannot sleep on the floor.'
'Why?'
'Because it's dangerous.'

'No, you cannot use the restrooms when the seat belt signs are on.'
'Why?'
'Because it's dangerous.'

'No, you cannot bring your friend from economy into first class.'
'Why?'
'Because they didn't pay for first class.'

'Madam, please return to your seat in economy.'
'Why?'
'Because you paid for economy, not business.'

'Just because I said so, because the captain said so, because it's the freakin' rules,' that was what she wanted to scream. Usually so calm and collected, Susan found her patience really being tried by these people tonight. She was pretty sure if she went into any of their places of work and they asked her to do something she would just do it, no argument, but up here, at 39,000 feet everyone had their own opinions!

'Cabin's secure,' she lied to the manager, Nick. Well she had told them all to fasten their seatbelts, if they chose to ignore her then so be it, they were grown adults and if they wanted to get hurt when the plane dropped five hundred feet then that was their choice! Except for the baby of course, that one she had gone back to check on, she cared about the poor mite even if the parents didn't seem to. She knew their indifference wasn't really about not caring, more desperation for their baby to sleep, but her short temper on today's flight was choosing to believe the worst of them.

Susan took a moment, breathing in deeply, trying to control her loathing that she suspected was more about herself than the passengers. She couldn't work out why she was so short-tempered this evening, going to New York, like she had done a thousand times before, but she had never felt this. Was it them or was it her? she asked herself over and over.

She wasn't seeing Tony this trip, not because she didn't want to but because she was flying into Newark and staying in a different hotel. She had only got back from her holiday two days ago and she wasn't quite ready to drop the wife and mother guise quite yet, wasn't sure she could be Susan Harrison quite so easily right now, after having such a lovely time with her husband. She had even managed to avoid Luke, and so her Mrs Kennedy hat was still well and truly on.

Ahhh! The penny dropped, *that* was why she couldn't tolerate these people tonight. Susan Kennedy didn't need to work. She didn't need to be here, doing this job, arguing with these people. *These* people didn't know who she was, how big her house was, how rich her husband was. Susan Harrison had no problem with them, never took things personally, always managed to win them round, but today the wrong Susan had come to work, and that wasn't a good thing!

'Any plans for New York, Susan?' Nick asked casually as they tidied the first class galley.

'No, actually, I haven't.' Susan realised at the same time as she told Nick that she had absolutely no plans, so mindless had her preparations for the trip been between unpacking from Dubai and packing for here. To be honest, she was quite looking forward to a night all on her own, in a bed without Jeff or anyone else in it. 'How about you?'

Before Nick had a chance to answer a call of, 'Help,' came from the cabin and they both rushed to see what had happened.

As their eyes adjusted to the darkness of the cabin Susan stopped just in time, before she tripped over the body that lay in the aisle.

'I'll get some oxygen,' said Nick calmly as Susan knelt down to raise the lady's feet.

Beth had already come from the next galley and shaken the lady, asking her name and making sure that she wasn't actually dead. Lucy recognised her from the seats further forward, confirmed when she turned around and saw her worried husband standing over them, face as white as his wife's.

'It's okay, sir, I think she's just fainted, it's quite common on flights,' Susan reassured him. It really was common, the combination of the lack of oxygen, and people's blood pressure dropping when they fell asleep meant that when they woke and stood up to go to the toilet they would often find themselves face down on the carpet. 'What is your wife's name, sir?'

'Carol,' he replied, already looking a little less worried now that the crew were there and his wife was starting to stir.

'Excuse me, sir.' Nick leant in past the man and passed Susan a bottle of oxygen. She turned it on and placed the mask over Carol's face. Seconds later the lady's eyes opened widely, shocked and confused to find herself on the floor with people that she didn't recognise peering down at her.

'It's okay, madam, you fainted,' Beth reassured her, and the lady nodded weakly, probably glad of the explanation of why she was where she was. 'Just stay there for a few minutes until you feel better.'

Susan could see blood trickling down the side of her face; she had clearly knocked herself on the way down, and she could now see a nasty cut above her eye.

'Nick, could you get the first aid kit please, I need to put something on that cut.' Susan was still holding the lady's legs up, getting the blood back to where she needed it, so tipped her head towards Carol's face. Nick saw what she was showing him, nodding before moving swiftly to the galley to locate what she needed.

What with the busy last service, and then the para-medics coming on board to see Carol when they landed, Susan hadn't given immigration a moment's thought. Not until she stood in line with the rest of the crew waiting for her turn to have her passport swiped.

# Chapter 34

'Right hand, four fingers,' he barked. Had he looked up he would have seen that her fingers were already on the machine, she knew the drill, for God's sake. He handed her back her passport and the crew declaration and she knew right away that she was off to secondary again, she could tell by the way his beady little eyes narrowed and the deep lines on his old, fat forehead got even deeper as he scowled at her. She snatched them off him and walked defiantly towards the baggage hall, knowing that the customs officer would take one look at the code he had scribbled and send her off to that room in which she didn't belong, again.

'Okay, who's coming out?' called Nick, leaning over his seat at the front of the bus and raising his hand.

Susan put her own hand up without hesitation. She had just endured another humiliating half an hour in secondary inspection, and was in need of something to loosen up the knots in her stomach. She struggled with it even more today than she had done before, probably because, like on board, she was still feeling like Susan Kennedy, and Susan Kennedy didn't even need to be here, let alone put up with this rubbish. Anyway, it was done now, and hopefully that would be the last time, as they had said her appeal could take up to a month to be processed. She wished she could actually make a complaint against Mark's wife, make her suffer a bit, but instead she had just pleaded that an error had been made, afraid of the can of worms she might open if it got personal.

She was glad that she always packed a 'just in case' outfit, even when she had no intention of going anywhere, you just never knew. There was no way she would be able to go out in her workout gear as she had seen plenty of girls do, when their plans of staying in their room and hitting the gym went awry, you just never knew who you would meet or what might happen.

'Any suggestions?' asked Nick.

'Flaming Saddles!' The answer came straight back, no hesitation, with murmurs of agreement. She looked around and noticed for the first time that day that the crew was made up heavily of boys, all of whom had their hands firmly up, and that could mean only one thing, they were going to a gay bar. She laughed inwardly, that was in fact perfect, with Susan Kennedy's hat still on she wasn't in the mood for hooking up with a stranger, so a bar full of men who had no sexual interest in her whatsoever was exactly what she needed! She was surprised to see that quiet and sweet Beth was the only other girl with her hand up, and she wondered if she knew what Flaming Saddles actually was? Regardless, she was glad to have another female on board, just in case the boys all left her as they fulfilled their own individual agendas.

The music was so loud in the bar that conversation was difficult, but it was fine as there was enough visual entertainment to be had with the eclectic mix of people in there. As they stood in their huddle watching the goings on around them, a roar of appreciation came from the direction of the bar. What must have been their signature song had started and the gorgeous boys that had just served them drinks catapulted themselves onto the wooden counter, launching straight into a well-rehearsed dance routine.

They may have been gay but that didn't stop the girls appreciating their toned bodies and dancing abilities, not one little bit, but while Susan's appreciation was more in her head, maybe given away by her smile, Beth's was much more obvious. They could only have had three drinks, but that was the equivalent of at least ten on landing day, and the Beth who stood next to her now bore no resemblance to the one who she had just flown over the Atlantic with.

'Whoop, whoop, go on, boys,' Beth called, circling her fist in the air, oblivious to the amused faces of the crew, all as shocked as Susan by her character change. She handed Susan her glass, promptly sticking two fingers from each hand into her mouth and blowing the loudest whistle she had ever heard. Susan caught Nick's expression as he too watched Beth, who was providing them with much more entertainment than the dancers were, and she fought to hold in the fit of giggles that was threatening to break out.

* * *

Their group had dwindled as the night wore on, leaving only Nick, Beth and Susan in the same spot as they had started. The others came and went, introducing them to various new 'friends' that they had just met, and Susan had lost track as the alcohol blurred her memory. The familiar roar came again and the bar staff were back on show, but it wasn't such a novelty now and she continued her conversation with Nick, talking loudly over the music. Suddenly Nick stopped her and put his hand on her arm, turning her around just in time to see Beth climbing onto the bar with gymnastic ability. The barmen made room for her, smiles fixed, trying to concentrate on their moves as Beth improvised her own in between them.

Within seconds Susan and Nick watched openmouthed as two burly security men carried their colleague unceremoniously from the bar and straight out into the street. They exchanged looks before leaving the bar themselves, by the same door that she had just been ejected from.

Outside Beth was still dancing, oblivious to the fact she had been thrown out and wouldn't be able to go back in, still high on the adoration of her fans, the crowds that, in her head, had been cheering for her.

'Time to go home I think, I'll get her back,' Susan laughed kindly, hailing a yellow cab.

'I'll come with you,' said Nick.

'No, it's fine, you stay put, I'm shattered anyway,' Susan insisted, as she was actually quite happy to go back now. Besides, she'd seen the way Nick had been exchanging looks with the young hot bartender who had been gyrating in front of them just minutes ago, it would be a shame to spoil his fun!

* * *

Nick waved them off, and as soon as the car began to drive Beth's eyes were closed and she was asleep, reminding Susan of her children when they were babies, and how the car would send them straight off. She felt maternal towards her colleague, and happy that she was able to get her home safely. As the cab drove back through Manhattan and towards New Jersey she looked through her window at the people who were going about their lives. As they turned down a small side street a familiar figure strode along up ahead, and when she looked to see who it was they'd passed she recognised Tony Carluccio, arm in arm with a beautiful brunette.

# Chapter 35

It was just like when she found out about Luke and Laura, seeing Tony with that girl had bothered her, and she was annoyed with herself for letting it do so. She wasn't stupid, she knew he must see other women, but it was always thousands of miles away, not in front of her. She wondered if whether had she told him she was in town, albeit in a different hotel, he would have come to see her instead of being with whoever that was? She liked to think that he would have, but her confidence was starting to falter lately, and she wasn't quite as sure of herself as she used to be, not quite so convinced of how irresistible she was anymore.

She thought it through; there was Luke, surely he didn't have any energy left for Laura now, what with his girlfriend and her? Then Tony, but he didn't even know she was in town, and perhaps he would have dropped everything for her if he had done. Mark, well she was pretty sure he was still infatuated, and Mario, well what about him? He was still available and playing by the rules. In fact, they all were, all still playing by the rules, *her* rules, she was the only one that wasn't right now, with her over-thinking and analysing.

She sipped her coffee, about to head to the gym, and scolded herself. She had to reset her mind, stop this madness, everything was still good, exactly as she liked it, wasn't it? She still had Jeff here, and Susan Harrison still had her men *there*, and that was how it was, how it worked. Perhaps Luke blurred the lines a little, but he was a separate entity, he was Susan Kennedy's secret pleasure, and surely she was allowed one?

Lucy came into the kitchen, head down, broom in hand, and distracted Susan from her justifications. She caught a waft of perfume that smelt vaguely familiar, realising that she had never noticed Lucy wearing perfume before. She studied her employee, who had her back to her now, and thought she looked different, her clothes a little nicer, her hair blow-dried and not just brushed as it usually was.

'You look nice today, Lucy,' she complimented her.

'Thank you.' Lucy didn't look up and Susan suspected she was embarrassed, not used to receiving them.

'And you smell wonderful, Lucy, what perfume are you wearing?' Susan asked, pushing Lucy to get into a conversation about herself, doubtful that she did very often.

'Um, I can't remember.' Lucy had stopped sweeping now, and turned around. 'Chanel, I think.'

'Oh yes, I thought I recognised it, one of my favourites,' Susan smiled at her, thinking how sweet it was that she was blushing, 'and I do believe you are wearing make-up, Lucy!' She didn't think she had ever seen her wear any obvious makeup before and the difference was quite striking. 'You look really lovely, Lucy.'

144

'Thank you, you're too kind.' She was smiling now, and standing up straight, confident, bolstered by the compliments.

'No honestly, Lucy, you look so lovely, not that you didn't before,' she added quickly, 'but even more lovely.' Susan finished the last of her coffee and put her mug in the sink. Lucy was still smiling, clearly loving the novelty of such nice things being said about her appearance. 'Right, I have to get to the gym, see you in a bit.'

'Okey doke,' Lucy replied cheerfully and went back to her work.

*I wonder if it's a man*, Susan mused as she drove away from the house, wondering what had brought on the change in her. It made her smile though, to see her make the most of herself and embrace her femininity. Lucy deserved a bit of happiness and she hoped that she had found it.


Lucy couldn't help smiling as she carried on with her work. Mrs Kennedy had been so kind with her compliments, and although for a brief moment she had felt guilty, it hadn't lasted for long. Guilt was nonsensical, pointless. Sure, Mrs Kennedy had smelt her own perfume on her, but she had no reason to suspect that Lucy had *borrowed* it, that it wasn't her own that she had simply had at home. Nor would she ever notice the few scraps of makeup that she had taken from her drawer, they were just ends of products after all, not the things she used, wasted, and Lucy appreciated them so much more herself. Even Mrs Kennedy had noticed what a difference a few choice things had made to her face after all.

She looked down at her clothes and sighed; that was

the only thing she knew she couldn't risk, but she so missed the designer wardrobe. Sure, she had made a few changes, buying a few nicer things, but she couldn't afford a lot, and the cheaper clothes just didn't do as much for her as the expensive ones had. Oh well, she couldn't have everything, not yet anyway, but maybe one day. She shook her head, trying to shake away the thoughts that had been coming these past weeks, despite the return of sleep. She knew they were wrong, that she shouldn't be having them, that despite her infidelity Mrs Kennedy was deep down a good person, but she couldn't help wanting this life, and imagining ways to get it.

# Chapter 36

Susan walked through the doors triumphantly, a sea of expectant faces looking at her. They were probably wondering what the crazy flight attendant was smiling at, it wasn't as if any of them were here to meet *her* after all. If only they knew, if only they had any idea how good it felt to be waved on through with the rest of the crew and not sent to that awful room like a convicted criminal, then they would be smiling this much too, she thought. Heck, it was all she could do not to skip! It looked like her appeal had worked and she was off the hook. Susan 1 - Mark's ex 0.

Perhaps she was being a little brave but she hadn't been able to resist telling him that she was coming here today either. Susan Harrison was quite looking forward to seeing her handsome man, the balance restored somewhat between her personas. It probably would have been sensible not to have seen Mark, to not risk upsetting his wife again, but then why should she? Besides, she needed his attention, his compliments and adoration, she needed her confidence back at its peak. The small victory in customs just made her surer that things were going right again, just how she liked them.

'Who's coming out for drinks?' asked the captain, as he handed out their room keys from the pile the receptionist had just given him.

'Sorry, I'm shattered. Early night for me,' Susan lied, trying her best to look weary.

'That's a shame,' he said. In her renewed confidence she thought that he looked disappointed but he recovered himself quickly and looked to the other girls for companionship. Susan quickly made her excuses and headed off to the lift, the others still making their arrangements in the lobby.

'Excuse me,' she heard, as a glamorous American lady jumped into the lift just as the doors were about to close. Susan smiled and moved aside to let her in. She was older than Susan, but still slim and dressed nicely, in the understated American way. Her hair was blow-dried big, reminding Susan of the eighties pictures her mum would show her, like the original Charlie's Angels.

The doors opened on the sixth floor and Susan stepped out. She was about to smile goodbye to the lady but she followed her, her room was clearly on the same floor. She pulled her case and crew bag behind her, looking for room 626, eventually reaching the last room in the corridor and holding her key against the lock to open it. She always hoped when she got the last room that it was a corner room, and she eagerly placed her case against the door to hold it open.

Not disappointed, she found her room was huge, with windows on two sides, and views across the bay, beautiful on this clear sunny day. She quickly checked for hidden attackers as per training, before returning to the door to retrieve her other bag. As she turned she noticed the lady from the lift still standing in the corridor a few rooms down, looking down at her phone with a serious expression on her face.

'Is everything okay?' Susan asked. She'd been stuck outside her room enough times when she'd forgotten her key, or when it had reset itself. The lady looked up from her phone. She seemed confused, as if the question had thrown her. 'Is your key not working? I can phone security to come up if you want?'

'Oh, um, no,' she stuttered, looking down and putting her phone back in her handbag, 'I'm fine, thanks.' She didn't smile, in fact she seemed annoyed, and Susan almost regretted asking if she was alright.

'Okay, well just knock if you need anything,' Susan offered, not sure what to make of her strange behaviour, but some Americans *were* a bit strange. Not all, but definitely some. She smiled at her anyway, and went into her room, closing her door behind her.... she had a bath to run and a good-looking man to prepare for.


Sitting in the penthouse lounge of the Intercontinental on Nob Hill, she thought the Top of the Mark cocktail bar was up there with some of her favourite places already. She quickly scanned through the list of speciality martinis, overwhelmed by the choice, her mind distracted still trying to take in the breath-taking views that were all around her. The city was getting dark and the lights outside were beginning to turn on, illuminating the landmarks and the edge of the bay. The Golden Gate

Bridge seemed to shine even more golden in the twilight across the water.

'I can't make up my mind, you choose one for me.' She handed the list to Mark, who she knew was a man of habit and would only drink the beer and brandy, making his own choice much easier than hers. He put up his hand to signal a waiter as he read them, obviously confident that his decision would be made before one arrived. It was one of the things Susan liked most about him, not only could he read people, but he could just see the answer in a split second, no matter what the question.

'I'm so sorry, Susan, that my ex-wife found out,' Mark said slowly, looking directly at her once the waiter had left. It was the first time that the whole matter had been mentioned, Susan not wanting to have the conversation in the confines of her hotel room when he had arrived. She obviously hadn't spoken to him at any length, and certainly hadn't mentioned her dramas with secondary search, but now that it was all over she found it almost comical to see this man who was always so in control hold his head in his hands, his face pulling horrified looks as she told him about each ugly time.

'I'm so, so, sorry.' His face had dropped, and he looked different somehow. 'I never knew she'd do anything like that. I can't believe she would be that way.'

'It's okay, honestly.' Susan felt almost sorry for him, needing to make him feel better so that he could return to his happy self. 'It's all over now, she's made her point, I'm sure she won't do anything else. Good job she's not FBI, hey, then I'd really have something to worry about,' she jested, trying to lighten the mood.

'I'm just so sorry.' He was leaning forward, elbows on

his thighs, and looked so cute looking up at her, forehead wrinkled, that she was pleased to see the waiter coming over with their drinks; it was time to change the conversation to something *much* lighter and end the poor man's suffering.

Hours later, fuelled by most of the martinis on the list, Susan clung to Mark's arm as they staggered down the steep hill back into town to her hotel. The evening had been fabulous and now she couldn't wait to get him back to her room.

The bellman tipped his hat at them as they passed him on the way to the lift, and once inside she hit the button to the sixth floor. She suddenly realised that she had forgotten to go in separately and was grateful that they hadn't been seen. The doors closed and Mark grabbed hold of her to kiss her, unable to wait until they were in the room, the tension too much. She took his hand as the bell signalled their arrival, and led him quickly down the corridor, fumbling in her bag for the room key.

With the door open Mark picked Susan up off the floor, carrying her over the threshold as if they had just married, and Susan laughed, probably too loudly for a hotel corridor, covering her mouth quickly.

The smell should have stopped them going any further but whether it was because they were laughing, and as such not breathing in deeply enough to notice it, or whatever, it was too late by the time that he had thrown Susan onto the wet bed to stop it happening.

Confused, Susan lay for a moment, hands feeling the

wet sheets around her, wondering if it was really possible that the smell of urine was coming from the bed on which she was lying or if she really had had too much to drink. Mark was standing at the end of the bed, having quickly jumped back after he too had noticed it.

'What the hell.' Susan got up, shocked and disgusted, Mark turning the bedroom light on to reveal a yellowing patch on the duvet, which coupled with its odour could only have been one thing. For the briefest of moments Susan was about to deny that it was her that did it, before realising that no one in their right mind would ever suggest that she had. The way that Mark was standing with his hand on his head, anger on his face, told her who did it, and that Mark knew exactly who it was too.

# Chapter 37

'Mark, show me a picture of your wife,' Susan ordered him as they caught the lift back to the lobby.

A look at the picture that Mark showed her confirmed what Susan was beginning to suspect; the glamorous American lady that had been in the lift with her earlier was Mark's wife. The realisation that she had actually managed to find out that she had flown in, find her hotel, and recognise her made Susan feel very uneasy, and almost relieved that all she had done was take a pee; the madwoman could have done something much worse!

The night had been ruined, obviously, and the embarrassment of Mark having to explain to the duty manager that his ex-wife had somehow got a key to her room, and peed on her bed was almost more than she could bear. She had insisted that he do it though. Why should she have to be embarrassed the next day when the maid cleaned the room to which *her* name was allocated, even if he paid for them to sleep elsewhere like he had offered? So, he had gone to the desk and explained, whilst she tried to sober up behind him, glad that these people were clearly on the night shift and wouldn't be around when she checked out. The shock on the young man's face was quickly replaced with a different look when Mark pointed out that one of his staff had given a complete stranger a key to Susan's room, and that the repercussions could have been so much worse. Susan was grateful for his insight, for distracting the focus from what *had* happened.


'Would you like us to call the police, ma'am?' Miguel, the manager asked her. She could see the look of hope in his eyes, hope that she would say no and he could go back to his easy night shift.

'That's not necessary,' Mark said quickly.

'Really?' Susan asked him, quite annoyed at how he had answered for her. Maybe, just maybe, *she* would like the filthy bitch to suffer for just a moment like she had done all those times in secondary, to understand that it was just *not okay, ever,* to pee on someone's bed! Susan shivered, unable to get away from the smell despite having scrubbed herself sore in the shower. 'Excuse us one moment,' she said curtly, taking Mark's hand and pulling him out of earshot.

'Mark, what the hell, you can't just let her get away with it!'

'I know, I know.' He was shaking his head, as if for the first time in his life he didn't know the answer.

'No, I want her to be arrested, Mark, it's not up to you, it's not you that she's stalking,' Susan said decisively. This time she wasn't letting him choose.

'Stop.' Mark grabbed her arm as she walked off, pulling her back. 'Look, I think the same, but if she gets arrested she'll lose her job, and if she goes to jail the kids lose their mom. Can we just hold fire? I promise I will sort it, she'll do what I tell her, and I promise you she will never bother you again.'

Mark was standing close, looking straight at her, and she believed him, believed that he would sort it out, whatever it took. Whilst she had no sympathy for *her*, the thought of the kids, who were utterly blameless in this messed up life that only Mark could take credit for creating, made her understand his reluctance. She nodded, defeated.

He had stayed that night, in a new room of course, but things weren't the same, and when he suggested they do something the next day, Susan had had to say it.

'Mark, I think it's best you go; go and sort your wife out, go and be with your kids.'

He looked at her, accepting, as if he had expected it.

'Will I see you again?' he asked as he left her room with his belongings. She just shook her head, sad to say the final farewell but knowing that there was no way they could carry on, things had got way too complicated, and that just broke all of the rules.


A few hours of retail therapy around Union Square did a bit to lift Susan's spirits. She hadn't wanted to end things with Mark, but she hadn't had a choice. She stopped for a pedicure in the small nail bar near the hotel, and as the Vietnamese lady massaged her feet, she closed her eyes and ran through the memories of Mark, from the day they had met. She felt like he had died, although she couldn't say she was grief-stricken, just sad.

As the afternoon turned to evening she felt tired and made her way back to the hotel. It was only 6pm, but 2am at home, and with the lack of sleep from the night before she was exhausted.

Susan put the key in the door and turned the light on before she let it shut. Despite years of checking her room for hidden attackers this was the first time that she had really taken her trainers seriously, for this time there was a real chance that someone *was* there.

She nearly screamed when she saw the object on the bed, unable to focus on what it was as her mind panicked, jumping back through the door and letting it close behind her. Her heart was racing, and she wondered what to do, whether she should call security to come up perhaps? Taking a deep breath, she put the key back in the door and pushed it open, again.

The object that had seemed so scary looked innocent now, a brown box with flowers on. She couldn't help but be nervous though, and propped her case against the door so that she could get out quickly should she need to, before going any further.

Slowly she approached it, reasoning that it was a harmless gift, probably an apology from Mark, confirmed when she took the lid off and to her relief was faced with the most beautiful bouquet of flowers. She took the card that was tucked into them and turned it over.

*To my beautiful wife*
*I miss you*
*Love Jeff*

Her eyes stung before welling up, and tears trickled down her cheek. What she would have done to be at home, with Jeff, safe in his arms in their lovely life at that moment. Why had she made things so difficult when she had everything that she could have wanted? Why was she risking it all for people who didn't matter? Why wasn't what she had enough for her?

*Go to sleep*, she told herself as she sank exhausted into her pillow, *you'll feel better in the morning.*

# Chapter 38

It was 8pm in California as the plane, a Boeing 787 Dreamliner, rumbled down the runway. Susan looked down over the city as they gained height, doubtful that she would be back for some time. She hoped that Mark would be able to sort out his wife, and deep down she knew that he would, that he would know what to say, or do, to stop her madness. Maybe they would get back together, and that thought made her smile, because actually, perhaps his family was as great as hers, he had just broken it because it wasn't enough, just like she had risked doing.

The seatbelt signs turning off signalled that it was time to get up, and Susan sighed at the thought of the long night ahead, grateful to be flying on the plane with the best crew rest area in the airline's fleet. The lights stayed dim in the cabin, the manager deciding not to wake the tired ones up too much, hoping that most would go to sleep.

'Did you have a nice trip, babe?' Liam asked as they prepped the drinks carts in the galley. She was working in the back tonight, and as much as she enjoyed working in first class she welcomed the ease of the service down here, the robotic nature of it, as opposed to the bowing and scraping that was required at the front.

'Yes thanks, just a quiet one,' she lied, cringing at the thought of the pee again. 'How about you?'

'Wish I'd had a quiet one, we ended up in Castro.' He rolled his eyes, he didn't need to explain to someone who had been there as long as Susan that Castro was *never* a quiet night.

'I'm skint and knackered.'

Susan laughed sympathetically.

'Oh dear, any regrets?' she asked, raising her eyebrows.

'I can't remember,' he said, pulling a puzzled face, and they both giggled.


Susan couldn't say if it was the passengers or the sub-par crew but the drinks service alone was like an uphill challenge. She had forgotten until they were boarding that this flight connected on to Bombay and Delhi, so perhaps it was just that she wasn't mentally prepared for an India flight and its unique challenges.

As she ran back to the galley for the twentieth cup of tea, with six sugars, she couldn't help but smile at the look of happiness it put on the lady's face, knowing that she was so far removed from walking in her shoes that she had no idea making a cup of tea was so much bother.

'Thank you,' she smiled sweetly.

'You're welcome,' Susan smiled back, resigning herself to ten minutes less in crew rest as a result of the extra-long service.

She was relieved as she pushed her cart into the galley,

but the feeling of acceptance she had just given herself was quickly lost when she saw the sides completely covered with special dietary meals piled five high.

Liam wiped a bead of sweat from his forehead as he turned and looked at her, marker pen in hand from writing the seat numbers on. His pained expression needed no words, and Susan just pulled the same face back. *Make that twenty minutes less*, she sighed inwardly.



Well, mistakes were bound to happen when you had sixty people eating special meals out of one hundred and fifty passengers. Perhaps someone had misread the seat number and given a vegetarian meal to the wrong passenger, who had accepted it anyway, but the man in the galley was adamant he had ordered one for his wife too, Liam confirming it on his list, but there were none left. Susan could see he was struggling, probably regretting his night out right now.

'This one's asleep.' Anna, the pretty young girl on her third flight, floated into the galley with a tray and everyone's eyes lit up. Liam snatched it off her quickly and handed it to the man, who shook his head from side to side and left seemingly satisfied, problem solved.



The upside to having given out so many special meals was that she was breezing down the cabin with very few people left to serve.

'How is your meal, madam?' she asked as she reached the man who had been in the galley, his wife tucking into her meal.

'Very good,' she smiled, 'this is paneer, no?'

Susan looked at the curry she was eating and felt her stomach flip, confirming her fear when she saw the label on the lid that lay on the side. The meal was a Muslim meal, not a vegetarian, and Muslims ate chicken....

'Yes, madam, enjoy.' She couldn't look at her and pushed her cart quickly on. Should she take it away now and admit that the poor lady was eating meat for the first time in her life, or just let her believe it was paneer and save her the upset? She decided on the latter and hoped that she would one day forgive herself. Anyway, wasn't that how she lived her two lives, on the assumption that what people didn't know didn't hurt them? No point getting all righteous now!

She finished up quickly, needing to get back to the galley and share what had happened with someone.

'You aren't going to believe this, hon,' she said to Liam, proceeding to tell him the whole ugly truth.

'Noooooo.' Liam's eyes were wide and he covered his mouth with his hand. She had to laugh, see the funny side now, especially looking at her colleague's horrified face.

'No one died, hon, and the engines are still turning,' she said, trying to get him to see that it wasn't the end of the world, the same things she had told herself these past few minutes, but he was still in the stomach flip stage that she had been in.

'I feel so awful, I didn't even look at the label, I just presumed...'

'We all did,' she said, trying to make him feel better, but relieved that he had pointed out it was actually his fault, so she had nothing to feel guilty about. Not this time, not here.

# Chapter 39

Susan didn't think that she had ever been so desperate to get home and see her husband, driving her Range Rover into her driveway. Winter was almost here and the house was starting to lose the colour that the flowers brought in the summer, but the warm yellow lights that shone out through the windows made it look all the more inviting, calling her to come in and be a part of it.

The events in San Francisco had really unsettled her, and she hadn't realised how much until she had woken up on the plane from the most vivid of dreams, scared. It had hit her once again that somebody had actually been able to follow her, and although what Mark's wife had done had been bad enough, it could have been much, much worse. She had to be grateful that it was all thousands of miles away now, and she had resolved in that moment of darkness in her crew bunk that all contact with Luke had to stop, that it was all too close to home. What if his girlfriend was as crazy as Mike's wife, what if she found out too? No, it must end now, she should never have let it start in the first place.

* * *

She hadn't expected it to be so easy, not that she had given too much thought to it, but as she drew up and parked her car he was walking across the garden with a leaf blower, fighting a losing battle with autumn.

*No time like the present*, she thought, determinedly, grateful that the colder weather had led him to cover up his toned body these past weeks.

'Luke,' she called, walking over towards him. He turned and smiled when he saw her.

'Welcome home,' he said, in recognition that she was still in her uniform.

'Thanks.' Susan was sure she wasn't looking her best but she didn't really care, knowing that he would quite happily meet her in the summerhouse if she suggested it right now. 'Luke, I need to talk to you, I need to say something and I need you to listen.'

'Listening,' he said slowly, looked confused and mildly amused at the same time.

Susan took a deep breath.

'We have to stop, you know,' she couldn't find the words, 'meeting up like we do.'

'Oh.' She thought he looked embarrassed. They had never really talked about their meetings, they just happened, and nothing had ever needed to be said. He looked at her earnestly. 'No worries, it was fun while it lasted.'

'Thank you, Luke.' She was relieved that he had taken it so well, not tried to persuade her otherwise, been grown up about it.

'It's just that I think we both have too much to lose,' she continued, feeling like she had to explain herself further, 'and it's too close to home.'

'It's okay,' he said kindly, 'you don't have to explain. I have to get on, I've got another job this afternoon.'

'Thanks,' she said, and turned to get her case out of her car.

'Let me know if you change your mind any time though.'

She turned quickly, seeing the cheeky grin on his face and couldn't help but smile back, shaking her head in amusement. That was the second time in as many days that she had ended things with someone and she felt her circle shrinking, but it was okay, she had enough right here. Susan Kennedy had enough.


She poured herself a glass of champagne, the children settled in their rooms, and looked at the kitchen clock. 8.30, he was sure to be home soon.

She felt smaller somehow, more vulnerable, like she needed a pair of big strong arms around her, and the only ones she wanted were her husband's, the one man who she could truly rely on. The flowers that she had carried all the way home on the plane were a testament to how he never forgot about her, even when she was so far away, like she did about him.

The sound of his car pulling up outside made her happy, and she jumped up to greet him, standing at the door beaming as he walked towards it.

'Now there's a sight for sore eyes.' She stretched out her arms and he enveloped her in his. 'What's all this for?'

'Nothing, I just missed you.'

'Well I'm glad to hear it but you don't normally miss me this much.'

It was true, she wouldn't normally stand at the door when he got back.

'Maybe after Dubai I just got used to being with you all the time,' she said innocently, leading the way into the lounge where she had set out some nibbles and the rest of the bottle of champagne she had opened.

'Dinner's in the oven,' she said, taking his jacket, stating the obvious. She was sure that he couldn't have missed the aromas coming from the kitchen, the meal she had spent hours preparing for him.

'Smells delicious, you look wonderful by the way.' Jeff had noticed the blue lace dress that she had picked out especially for his appreciation. It was one of the things she had taken on board in Dubai, how the ladies in their burkas wore beautiful dresses underneath, but only for their husband's eyes, not for other men to ogle.

'Thank you.' It hadn't been the dress she had planned on wearing, but that one was nowhere to be found, despite looking high and low. She was sure she had seen it before they went away, almost taking it with her, but now it couldn't be found anywhere, strangely. Anyway, it wasn't as if she hadn't had plenty of other choices but it was odd nonetheless. 'You put your feet up and I'll get dinner ready.' She blew him a kiss over her shoulder as she left the room, an unspoken promise for the night ahead.

# Chapter 40

Lucy stood in front of her mirror admiring how the dress that she had *borrowed* from Mrs Kennedy made her look, especially teamed with the expensive shoes that she had paid for on her new credit card. She would put the dress back after the party, but she needed it this weekend, more than her boss did. She knew Mrs Kennedy wouldn't notice it was missing, it was just one of a hundred in her closet, after all.

Tonight, she had been invited to a dinner party at Kate James's house. She had been so shocked by the invitation that she hadn't thought it through before saying yes, that she'd love to come, and meet all of her lovely friends! Now she was getting nervous, but the dress made her feel better, and she reasoned that if she looked good then she would feel good.

She was starting to feel better in herself lately, the medication that the doctor had given her was definitely helping, and with the return of sleep the dark thoughts were going now. She was glad for that, happy to not have the voices that made her jealous and think bad things, especially those about her boss. It helped that she suspected whatever had been going on between her and her nephew was over, she had been watching them closely, but there had been no meetings in the summerhouse, or anywhere else, that she was aware of lately.

As for her needing her life, those thoughts were weaker now too, she was quite happy back home as her old self, most of the time. She actually wished that she had never met Kate that day, that she had never reinvented herself in her madness to this rich person. Now she had to keep it up or she would be ridiculed by the same people that had made fun of her at school, the Natashas that for the moment thought she was as good as them, better even.

She caught the frown on her face in the mirror and shook herself, looking at her reflection and finding the pleasure in her façade. No harm was being done, and it felt good that they believed that she was rich and glamorous. She laughed to herself at the ridiculousness of it, their gullibility and shallowness, and felt justified. Despite her sanity she was going to be an actress tonight and enjoy their admiration, only she would know her truths.


'Thank you,' Lucy said as Natasha filled her glass, again. This was the third time she had caught her doing it, and she had no idea how many other times there had been, the champagne never seeming to go down in the crystal flute. She could feel the effects of the bubbles, her confidence growing as she *really* began to get into character.

She was sitting at one end of the sofa in a room that could have come straight from the pages of a Laura Ashley home magazine. Everything in it just seemed to go perfectly with everything else, and she wondered if Kate had paid someone to put it all together. Back home in her flat things had just been added to over the years, a mixture of old and new, sentimental and just quirky. She knew that the Kennedys had had interior designers, and so had never compared her style to theirs, but she suspected that Kate was naturally able to create spaces like this, that just made you in awe of them. The house, while not huge like where she worked, was still substantial, and now that she was sitting here with these people, who probably all lived in similar properties, she was conscious not to let her mask slip.

'It was absolutely my favourite ever holiday, The Atlantis is just out of this world.'

'Oh, it sounds wonderful, I'll definitely have to look into it.' Kate had been listening intently to Lucy's description of her holiday in Dubai. The truth was, she only knew what she had read in the brochure that Mrs Kennedy had left behind, but right now even she believed that she had been there.

'Oh, you must, everybody should stay there at least once.' She took a sip of her champagne.

'So, Lucy, when are we coming around to yours, I've been telling everyone about your lovely house.' It felt like everyone was looking at her, all these people who she didn't know, who believed she was rich and confident, as Natasha asked the question.

'I will organise something soon, that would be lovely. Yes, what a fabulous idea, Natasha.' Lucy wondered if the Kennedys would be asking her to housesit again any time soon, but she doubted it. Oh well, she didn't have to *actually* organise anything, just say that she would and forget about it.

'When?'

Lucy took a big sip of her drink, wishing that Natasha would just change the subject now. Still everyone was looking at her, all with fixed smiles, seeming to lean in towards her, waiting for her answer.

'Um, well,' *think, quick*, 'Well it can't be the next couple of weeks as we are having some work done, I'll let you know.'

Phew, that was close, she hoped she had done enough, said enough to stop her now.

'Well don't forget, or I'll be calling in on you without the invite.' Natasha laughed and Lucy saw the old Natasha, the bully who always pushed people into doing what she wanted. Oh heavens, what was she going to do? Another glug of champagne and she managed to laugh at the loaded joke.

'Don't worry, I won't forget.' How could she possibly forget, with the threat of them turning up uninvited and uncovering her lies? She couldn't let that happen, it would be unbearable.

As the taxi drove her home Lucy finally let the smile drop, and felt the panic that she had managed to suppress begin to rise. What on earth was she going to do? She hoped that Natasha would just forget, but she suspected that she wouldn't, and it wasn't a risk that she was willing to take. She pictured the worst-case scenarios of them arriving unannounced to find out that she was just the cleaner, and it made her feel quite nauseous. No, she would have to think of something, a way to get the house to herself, just for an evening, once the champagne fog had lifted.

# Chapter 41

Over two weeks had passed since Susan had got back from San Francisco, and she had made a conscious effort to put the memories of the whole thing to the back of her mind. The comfort of being back with her family had settled her immensely, and for a few days that had been enough for her, but now she could feel herself getting uneasy, the mundane becoming almost suffocating.

'See you tonight.' Jeff kissed her quickly, grabbing his jacket from the back of the dining chair and heading for the door, off to work.

'See you tonight,' she echoed, hiding the disdain in her voice as he took another pastry from the glass cake stand on his way out. Ever since they had gotten back from holiday he had completely given up on the diet, and the exercise, and she could see the extra pounds starting to stack back on him. She wished he was enough for her, that she didn't have these urges for excitement that he just wasn't able to satisfy. It wasn't that she hadn't tried to spice things up, to find what she needed with her husband, but it was just boring, and he never seemed that interested anyway these days, not as often as she wanted him to be now that she was limiting her other sources. Maybe when she reached his age she too would be happy just to cuddle up at night, and perhaps he misread her mirroring of his actions as her being content to be like this. But she wasn't, not yet.

'Come on then, you two, let's get you to school.'

The two children looked up from their devices, empty breakfast bowls in front of them, taking a second to understand what she had said before moving to get up.

'Mum, can Lily come round after school?' Sophia asked as she put on her coat and shoes.

'I don't see why not, we don't have any plans,' Susan said, pleased at the smile that her answer put on her daughter's face. She pulled on her own leather boots, and checked her appearance in the mirror; no gym today as she had a hair appointment, and it wouldn't do to turn up looking less than lovely, appearances always needed to be kept up.

'Can you ask her, Mum?' Sophia asked sweetly.

'I don't have her number, darling.'

'You can ask her in the playground.' It was like her daughter had pre-empted her answer, knowing her reluctance to talk to the other mums unless she really had to.

'Okay,' Susan agreed, 'but can't you just message her?'

'Muuuum,' Sophia said, clearly frustrated with her social inability.

'Okay, okay.' It wasn't that she wasn't able to speak to people, it was just that she always felt like they were judging her, especially when they saw her in her uniform, thinking that they were better, looking down on her.

* * *

'She's over there,' Sophia pointed to the group of mums across the playground, 'the one in pink jodhpurs.'

Susan groaned, it was the horsey group. The ones who smelt of hay and horses, and wore jodhpurs every day like a badge of honour. She wondered if they actually all owned horses, or if some just pretended in order to fit in with those who did. Some of them just really shouldn't wear such trousers over their generous bottoms, she thought critically, feeling sorry for their poor ponies.

She took a deep breath as she approached them, not making it obvious that they were her target group until she was right next to them, not wanting their attention any longer than was necessary. She held on tightly to Sophia's hand, needing her daughter's back-up.

'Hi,' Susan smiled as her target turned around and looked up at her. The woman couldn't have been more than five feet tall, and reminded her of the curvy cartoon character with the horse from her childhood. She didn't wear a scrap of makeup, and her wiry hair was in desperate need of some TLC, and yet it was she who was looking at Susan critically. She wasn't imagining it, she actually looked her up and down, and the smile that she had been wearing for the rest of the group left her face. In true flight attendant style, Susan however was still smiling, confident that her own derision was not showing. 'Sophia was wondering if Lily could come around after school.'

'Oh, well I'll have to see if she has any commitments,' she replied slowly and seriously, reminding Susan of an old teacher she once had.

The bell rang and Susan felt Sophia pull her hand out of hers, running off to her classroom. Without her she felt exposed, and it seemed like the whole group were now looking at her, from head to toe and back up again. Susan disliked them all even more now that she had met them up close, the nasty, judgmental bitches.

'Okay, well I'll be collecting Sophia later so I'm happy to collect Lily too, just let me know.' She took out a pen from her bag and scribbled her number on a piece of paper, holding it out to Lily's mum. She turned the moment it left her hand, not even saying goodbye, knowing that they were all watching her walking away now, talking about her. Oh well, let them look, she told herself as she always did, they could judge but then so could she, and she knew whose life she would rather have.

The smugness that she normally held inwardly was short-lived, and her pace slowed as it dawned on her that she wasn't much more exciting than any of them right now. Yes, her husband was rich, but so were theirs. She couldn't even presume he was any better looking either, not now he was getting comfortable again. Even Susan Harrison was losing her edge. The thought that she no longer had many reasons to be secretly smug was an unwelcome realisation, and unsettled her; maybe she needed to swap her next flight for a Miami, maybe a night with Mario was just what she needed to put things back in the right balance again.

# Chapter 42

'Mum, can I sleep over at Lily's next weekend?'

Susan looked up from the vegetables that she had been chopping on the kitchen island, preparing the dinner. Lily's mum had messaged her at lunchtime, obviously unable to think of any excuse to keep her daughter away, and now here they both were, already planning their next event.

'I'm going to ride her pony.' Sophia was wide-eyed with excitement.

'What does your mum say, Lily?' Susan asked the girl who looked so small next to her daughter, obviously already taking after her mum in the height department.

'She says it's fine,' she said casually, looking past Susan. 'Who's that?'

Susan turned around to see Lucy at the sink scrubbing away at something; she had forgotten that she was even in the kitchen with her.

'That's Lucy,' she said matter-of-factly, *and that is all the information you are getting, nosey*, she thought. She wasn't about to belittle Lucy by giving the girl her job title, not that she really knew what that was, and besides it was none of her business. Lucy didn't even turn around.

'Thanks, Mum.'

'Actually …' Sophia was just about to run off when Susan realised a potential problem. 'I forgot I've just swapped onto a flight this weekend, I'm not sure if Dad will be able to drop you off on Friday, it depends when he finishes work.'

'I can drop her off.' Lucy's voice startled Susan somewhat, she had thought that she hadn't been listening to the conversation, and she turned to see her, hands still in the sink, turning around from the waist up and smiling at her. 'I'll be picking them up, I presume, if you're flying anyway?'

'It's okay, my mum can bring Sophia straight back with us after school,' Lily stated the obvious solution.

'Yes, that makes sense, but if you could pick Lewis up for me, Lucy, that would be great. Sorry, I had meant to mention it to you but I only changed the flight this afternoon.' She realised how much she actually took Lucy for granted and felt bad for a moment. 'Would you be okay to stay on until Jeff gets home?'

'Of course.' Lucy looked quite happy to be asked, and Susan's moment of guilt passed, she always made sure she was squared up for these extra hours after all.

'That's sorted then, girls, just let Dad know what time to pick you up, Sophia, and he'll need Lily's address.'

The girls ran off happily back upstairs, the sound of their footsteps like thunder from the hallway.

'Thank you, Lucy, for always being so flexible.'

'Oh, it's no problem at all,' she replied, turning away again, back to scrubbing whatever it was that was so dirty.

* * *

Susan ran lightly up the stairs, the children safely occupied eating their tea. Not only had she only just told Lucy, but she hadn't yet told the most important person about her new plans yet.

She reached into the handbag at the back of the closet and pulled out the phone that lived there, turning it on.

*I'll be out on Friday, are you free?* she texted.

She held her breath for a moment, unsure how she would take a negative response. She *needed* Mario to be free this weekend, Susan Harrison needed to replace the last memory that she had with a good one, and Susan Kennedy needed a break so that she could come back refreshed and able to be great again, with her confidence back.

*Sure am!*

Oh, the relief of the quick response, and its content!

*See you then*

She quickly turned the phone off and put it back into the bottom of the bag, feeling the smile on her face stretching wider than it had done for a while. As she stood back up she took a moment to compose her excitement before leaving the closet, looking mindlessly around. A hanger poked out slightly from the neat rows of dresses and she reached out to straighten it.

*That's odd*, she thought, as she recognised the dress that she couldn't find just the other day. She was positive she had looked through that rail at least three times and it definitely wasn't there. She shrugged her shoulders. Oh well, it was there now, she must have missed it after all, she tried to persuade herself, but she wasn't quite convinced.

# Chapter 43

She hadn't seen Luke for a while, his hours shorter now that winter was looming and the garden didn't need as much work, and she took a moment to admire him from a distance as she stood on her doorstep, case in her hand. She could feel Susan Harrison bursting to get out, and she walked quickly towards her car before she did something stupid. The kids were safely deposited at school, Jeff was at work, and she was ready and raring to go.

'Have a safe flight,' called Lucy cheerily, closing the front door and waving.

'Thanks again for everything, Lucy,' she called back. Not only had she offered to pick up Lewis from school but she had also agreed to stay on late so that Jeff could meet some clients after work. In fact, it had been her suggestion yesterday, one that Jeff had jumped at, always happy to avoid coming straight home to the kids and being on his own when she was away. Only Lewis was left, and she knew he would be more than happy to be left to his own devices in his room, Lucy wouldn't even know that she had him.

She beamed as she drove through the gates; everybody was going to have a lovely weekend, including her.

Damn it! Susan's mood was sinking as she sat in traffic that hadn't moved for the past twenty minutes. She was sure that someone further up was having a much worse day than her, especially if, as she suspected, an accident had caused the tailbacks. Even so, in her world things were starting to look bleak too. She had to be at check in in forty-five minutes, and although she only had a few miles to go, at this speed it could take hours. She swung between anxiety about making the flight, and sympathy for the people who were possibly injured up ahead, as more blue lights flashed past her along the hard shoulder.

The car that was upside down in the outside lane about a mile further up was testimony to how bad a day could really get, and Susan couldn't help slowing down to look as she passed. Then it was gone, and as all of the lanes of the motorway opened up ahead of her, she put her foot down hard on the accelerator. With only ten minutes to go there was no way she would make it, but she hoped they would let her go straight to the aircraft and not roll her onto the next flight, as the lady in scheduling had suggested they may.

'Just make your way and let us know when you're at the terminal, then we'll see what we'll do,' she had said, sympathetic but not at all helpful. If she wasn't going to Miami then quite frankly she'd rather just go home, where she could be miserable and disappointed on her own, not on a plane full of people going to somewhere she didn't want to go! Besides, the bikini and sun dresses she had packed would be of no use to her if she ended up somewhere cold!

She practically screeched into the parking space, jumping out and grabbing her small case from the back seat just as the bus pulled up at the bus stop. Normally she wouldn't have shamed herself by running, but these were desperate times, and she didn't care as she ran awkwardly in her heels, not even taking the time to put her case on the ground and still carrying it. The relief when she caught the driver's eye, knowing that he had seen her, and that only a complete git would drive away now, was enough to let her slow up, hoping to regain her dignity before getting onto the crowded vehicle. It was short-lived dignity though, as she tripped on the step and found herself falling backwards, landing star-fished on her back at the foot of the bus door.

She knew that the driver wanted to laugh as he looked down at her from his seat through the doors that she had been about to enter through. She probably would have been the same, but she was grateful beyond words that he didn't.

'Are you okay, love?' he asked, as she quickly stood up and brushed herself down.

'Fine, thanks,' she replied, taking a deep breath before stepping onto the bus. Why, oh why, did it have to be so packed? she cried on the inside, walking past the people who too were trying not to laugh, to the only empty seat at the back. Only once she was seated did she notice the pain in her ankle and the graze on her wrist, and she could only hope that the day got better from here. At least she had made the bus, she thought, pleased to finally find the silver lining.

* * *

By the time she arrived at the aircraft door the passengers were boarding, and she squeezed past, emulating the fixed smiles of the crew who were standing there. She recognised one of them, a girl called Dani who she'd flown with a few times before, remembering her for being very relaxed in her attitude to work. She made her way to the front of the plane to introduce herself to the manager and find out where she was working. Her ankle was really throbbing now, and she was trying desperately not to limp, in case someone noticed and sent her home again if they deemed her unfit to fly. A few painkillers would help when she got a chance to take them.

The manager was standing in the front galley reading through the paperwork that the ground staff had just given her, and didn't even look up when Susan walked in.

'Hi, sorry I'm late, I'm Susan.'

'Oh, glad you made it.' The young girl who could only have been in her late twenties looked up and smiled at her. She was possibly the youngest flight manager that Susan had ever seen, and was extremely beautiful, with a dark exotic look. 'Go and get yourself a drink, hon, and have a minute, everything's done.'

Susan could have hugged her for her kindness, the stresses of the last two hours starting to ebb away.

'Thank you so much, I've had a hell of a time getting here, where am I working?' She glanced at her name badge. *Sheena, what a pretty name*, she thought.

'Down the back, but there's only fifty passengers so you'll have an easy night.' She smiled as she delivered the good news.

'Amazing!' It must have been a pre-Christmas lull in travelling. Whatever it was, Susan would have skipped down the empty aisles had her ankle allowed her to. The passengers were hard to spot in the empty seats and her day had suddenly got better.

# Chapter 44

Lucy couldn't believe her luck with how things had worked out. The moment that Mr Kennedy had accepted her offer for him to stay out late she had messaged Kate and Natasha to come round for wine and canapés.

*Bring a few friends*, she had added, hoping that it wouldn't be too many, before mentioning that she would have to wrap things up by eleven as they had an early start in the morning. She couldn't risk them getting too comfortable and staying past then, as she would need to make sure all traces were gone by the time her boss got home, and from previous experience that would be by the last train just after midnight. She couldn't help feeling nervous that he would come back early, but she would have to live with the butterflies as tonight was necessary. At least there was no chance of Mrs Kennedy coming back, she had waved her off to the airport this morning so she was long gone.

The afternoon had been filled with preparations. A small fortune spent in M&S, on the credit card that was starting to get out of control. Removal of family pictures from the walls, and other signs that might give her away should they nose around the house. It occurred to her that she hadn't thought about that the last time Kate and Natasha came over, and she realised how lucky she had been that they hadn't noticed. Lewis had been bribed already with unlimited sweets and screen time to stay in his room, and she wouldn't let anyone go upstairs unless she went with them; even Natasha wouldn't be able to bully her into letting her snoop around.

The final part of her plan was the non-alcoholic champagne she had bought for herself. She couldn't afford to lose any control tonight, she just had to get through it, and she wouldn't be able to if she was in the same state she had been in by the time she had left Kate's!


'You look lovely, Lucy, I *love* that dress,' gushed Kate as she greeted her at the front door.

'Thank you.' Lucy took the compliment, pleased with the green dress that she had chosen from Mrs Kennedy's wardrobe tonight.

Natasha walked in next, kissing Lucy on the cheek, followed by two of the ladies that she had met at Kate's. She had no idea of their names, noting merely that one was blonde and one brunette; since they were never going to be friends it was pointless to learn them now.

'Come on in, lovely to see you all again.' Lucy surprised herself at how naturally she took to the role of the rich hostess. She would never have been this confident and assured in her own clothes, at her own home. But there was nothing here that they could judge her on, nothing negative anyway.

'Please, go through to the living room.' Lucy gestured

towards the lounge, where she had set up her over-priced nibbles. 'I'll be through in a second with some bubbly.'

'Do you need a hand?' offered Kate.

'No thanks, I have it all under control, I'll just fetch a cold bottle.'

Lucy moved swiftly into the kitchen, taking a bottle of champagne from the chiller and quickly filling her own glass with the non-alcoholic version that would stay hidden in the fridge. She would have to keep an eye on Natasha in case she took to filling up her glass like last time.

'Right, who's for a glass of champagne?' Lucy announced, filling the glasses that she had set up on the coffee table.

'Ooh yes please.' The petite brunette girl whose name she couldn't remember jumped up without hesitation. 'Lucy, this is such a beautiful house.'

'Thank you.' It felt completely okay to accept the compliments that just kept coming.

'Do you mind if we have a look around?'

Lucy paused momentarily from pouring the champagne. She had expected the question, and rehearsed how she would deal with it, but it still made her stomach flip nonetheless.

'Of course, just let me fill these and I'll give you a tour.' She looked up and smiled, making eye contact; no one would be 'looking around' without her.


'This is the kitchen, obviously.' Lucy showed the four girls into the room. Kate and Natasha had been here before of course, but were happy to be shown again.

'Wow, look at that garden.' The nameless blonde girl was peering through the window at the garden. It was lit up theatrically in the darkness, with carefully placed lighting showing off the pool and the summer house. 'It must be wonderful in the summer.'

'Oh, it is, we love it out there.' She looked over towards the dogs who were lying on their beds at the far end of the room.

'It must take a lot of keeping up though, do you have a gardener?'

'Yes, a lovely lad called Luke takes care of it, he does an amazing job.' Lucy wanted to add that she was his proud aunty but thought better of it.

'Oh, we have a gardener called Luke too!' she exclaimed, 'I wonder if it's the same one? Luke Wright?'

Lucy heard her pulse in her head as her heart rate quickened; she had to think really quickly, this was a possibly really bad situation.

'Oh no, it can't be the same one, *our* Luke only works for us as he has a full-time job as well.'

'Oh, well Luke is obviously a good gardener's name,' she quipped. 'My Luke is quite talented in other departments too.' She giggled, looking down at her glass, and her friend obviously knew what she was talking about as she was stifling a laugh too.

It suddenly dawned on Lucy what she meant and she felt her cheeks flush. She could feel herself getting angry and tried to push it back, she would have to process all of this later when she was on her own.

'Oh, well our Luke just does his job.' She forced a smile, but inside she was seething, her nephew was clearly a complete slut who was sleeping with every lonely housewife that he worked for. Clearly Mrs Kennedy wasn't the only one.

'Can we have a look upstairs, Lucy, we didn't get to see that last time?' It was Natasha, exactly as she had predicted it would be, pushing things one step further out of her comfort zone.

'Of course, but a couple of the rooms are off limits as they are where my husband works from home, and I've also got my nephew to stay so he's in bed already.' She had considered excuses to completely put the upstairs out of bounds, but as she had been getting ready in the Kennedys' suite she hadn't been able to fight the pull to show off this wonderful room as her own. The quick explanation about her nephew had her covered just in case Lewis came out of his room or made a noise, as much as she doubted that he would.

'And this is where the magic happens,' she winked. Such a comment was completely out of character for the real Lucy, but hey this one right here had everything, so she may as well have a great love life as well. She could feel the envy from them all as they looked around the room and the bathroom, making sounds of appreciation.

'I'm afraid that's all I can show you up here.' She led them back to the top of the stairs. 'Please, go on down and fill your glasses up. I'm just going to check the windows are closed in the study, be down in a second.'

She stood at the top and ushered them down the stairs, before heading to Lewis's room and quietly opening the door. As usual he was on the floor with his back to her, headphones on and controller in hand. She walked over and tapped him on the shoulder.

'Into bed soon, young man.'

'I'll just finish this game,' he said sweetly, turning and giving her a thumbs up. She gave him a thumbs up back, glancing at her watch as she did so. Nine o'clock, just two more hours to get through.

# Chapter 45

As was often the way with the quiet flights, time could really drag. There was only so many times you could offer drinks, or check the toilets. The positive side was that the crew had been split in half and given four hours' rest each, so at least she would be arriving into Miami nice and fresh. The pain in her ankle had subsided, thankfully, once the painkillers had kicked in, and she would *not* be going out in flats after all!

'Is the crew food cooked?' Sheena walked into the galley, surprising Susan. She had got on the plane in such a rush, and what with going straight into taking off and the dinner service, she had actually forgotten who the manager was until she saw her again.

'Yep, in the first two ovens.' Susan looked up from the magazine she had been flicking mindlessly through. 'Don't get too excited though.'

'Oh, I won't!' Sheena knew what Susan was getting at, the crew food not being the most interesting of menus. She pulled out each of the drawers, looking for inspiration, before taking something out. 'Baked potato.'

'I know, it really is dire today. Was there nothing left at the front?'

'Nope, we ran out of everything except the fish, and I didn't fancy that. New menu.'

'Aaah.' Susan knew what she meant, the ratios were never right when there was a new menu. 'Baked potato it is then!'

'Oh, the glamorous life of a flight attendant,' Sheena laughed, peeling back the foil from her veritable banquet, putting it into a bowl. 'Are you going out with everyone tonight?'

'Probably not, are you?' It was the usual 'what are you doing this trip' question, but worded in a way that suggested that she wasn't either.

'No.' She had her back to Susan as she prepared her dinner on the galley side. Susan was surprised that this glamorous young thing wasn't going out in Miami, but everyone had their own agendas. 'I'm with the first officer, between me and you, so we are just going to go out for dinner.'

'Oh, I didn't realise, that's nice.' She gauged that not everyone was privy to this information by how she had said it, that they were keeping it to themselves for whatever reason. Susan hadn't had a chance to get up to the flight deck, what with arriving so late, and now with so few crew on duty it wasn't sensible to leave the cabin unattended, so she hadn't seen who the first officers were. In fact, she realised that she didn't even know the name of the captain, which was pretty poor, and would have been frowned upon by higher powers.

'Yep, it's only been a few months so we're keeping it a bit quiet, but it's nice to get on a flight together.'

'Of course,' Susan agreed. She had never had anything meaningful with a pilot, not that she couldn't have done if she had wanted, but she had always preferred to have her beaux across the Atlantic permanently.

'Anyway, I'd better go back up, let me know if you need anything.'

'Thanks, I think we should be okay though,' she said dryly. It was like a ghost ship in economy and she was pretty sure she and Dani could just about manage. 'Dani's just popped to the loo.'

'Well you know where I am.' Sheena gathered up her food and covered it with a napkin.

'Thanks,' Susan said just as her colleague walked back into the galley.

'Sorry I was so long, a lady up by the toilets isn't feeling too good.'

'What's up with her?' Susan asked, Sheena stopping in her tracks.

'I'm not really sure, she just feels a bit queasy. I've given her some water and told her to press her call bell if she starts to feel any worse.'

'Okay, well keep an eye on her, and call me at the one-doors if you need me,' Sheena said.

'Will do.' Dani didn't seem worried by the situation at all.

'Shall we take turns to watch a movie?' Dani asked with a mischievous look, once Sheena was out of earshot.

'Hell yeah,' Susan didn't need persuading, 'first or second?'

'First if it's alright with you?'

'Of course, I'll hold the fort and keep a look out.' Not that she thought Sheena was likely to come back any time soon.

'Perfect, I'm just going to slip into the last row.' Dani took her bottle of water from the side. 'Oh, it's row 48 by the way, just in case she presses her call bell.'

'Perfect, I'll check on her in a bit,' Susan assured her, glad to have something to do, regardless of how small, to pass some time.

The poor lady didn't look well at all, and Susan instantly took pity on her as she passed her with a tray of drinks.

'Madam, how are you feeling?' she asked as sympathetically as she could.

'Terrible, I think it's something I ate.' She rubbed her stomach.

'Why don't you lie down?' There were countless empty rows for her to move into.

'I tried, but it was too uncomfortable with the armrests.'

She was a bigger lady and Susan supposed that although the armrests went up, they would still dig into her back.

'Oh dear, you poor thing.' She looked like she wanted to cry and Susan's maternal side just wanted to hug her.

'I'll be back in a minute.' She turned and walked quickly to the front of the plane.

'Have you seen Sheena?' she asked the crewmember that she was seeing for the first time now, in the galley. She was flicking through the same magazine that Susan had been earlier.

'No, babe, I presume she's on the flight deck, she seems to like it in there.' She gave Susan a knowing look. Susan wondered why Sheena had chosen to share that information with her and leave other crew to speculate. Maybe because she was older, or not working in the same galley.

'Okay, thanks.' She walked quickly through the almost empty first class cabin, the whole plane was deserted it seemed. Just as she was about to put the code into the keypad and request access to the flight deck, the door to the pilot's crew rest area opened to her side. Sheena looked surprised to see Susan standing outside and appeared embarrassed.

'Is everything okay?' she asked, failing at acting casual, shutting the door quickly behind her. Susan thought she had seen another figure in the small room behind her, and coupled with Sheena's slightly unruly hair, made the pretty safe assumption that she hadn't been in there alone.

'Um yes.' She tried to compose herself, to not show the amused shock on her face or in her voice. 'I was just wondering if I could bring our poorly lady up and put her in a bed, she is so uncomfortable down there and I think she'll be better off lying down.'

'Yes, yes, of course.' Susan suspected that Sheena would have agreed to most things just to end this awkward moment.

'Fabulous, I'll go and get her and pop her in 8K.'


As Susan put the very sick but very grateful lady to bed a few minutes later, she glanced up the cabin to see a familiar figure quietly leaving the pilots' rest area, the same one from which her manager had just come. Ray, him from Chicago, with the red-hot abs, was running his fingers through his hair and fastening his tie. *Well, well, well*, Susan thought, doing the maths quickly, *he's definitely not one for monogamy*. Poor Sheena, she hoped she wasn't as naive as she looked.

# Chapter 46

This was harder than she thought it would be, Lucy thought despairingly as the time seemed to stand still. The girls were all very merry on Mrs Kennedy's expensive champagne, and being the only sober one just wasn't helping the situation. She kept the smile on nonetheless, making sure that she was a perfect hostess and that they would have no reason to criticise her when they left.

'Selfie time,' squealed Natasha.

Everyone squeezed in behind her, grinning with their perfect teeth.

'And you, Lucy, c'mon.'

Lucy reluctantly took her place behind them, wincing at her image in the camera screen. All the others seemed to know exactly which way to tilt their heads, and how to show just the right amount of teeth and gum, but Lucy was clueless in the whole thing, and didn't have the luxury of experimenting now.

Click.

'Perfect,' said Natasha as they gathered around to see how they would look on whichever social media account they were going to be put on. 'What's your Instagram name, Lucy?'

'Um.' Lucy wondered what she was talking about for a moment, before the penny dropped. 'Oh, I don't have any of that,' she said, and wasn't that a good thing, she thought. Everyone had gone quiet and they were looking at her as if she was mad.

'Erm, why not?' Natasha obviously couldn't fathom it, there needed to be an explanation for her abstinence.

'I just never bothered,' Lucy said matter-of-factly. She was sober enough not to let the increasingly drunk Natasha bully her now.

'Christ, if I had all of this I'd be putting pictures of it up left right and centre,' she said, waving her hands around at the room.

Lucy was hugely grateful that she didn't have any social media now, *that* would really have added to this whole problem. She was tiring of the whole act, and just wanted the night over so that she could distance herself from them all again and go back to her quiet, peaceful life.

'Oh, I'm getting ever so tired,' she yawned and looked at her watch; it was only ten o'clock but maybe they would take a hint.

'Any more bubbles, Luce?' Kate asked, tipping the last dregs from the bottle she had only just opened into her glass.

'Oh yes, of course.' Lucy got up, relieved to have a break from their giggling and childishness for a moment.

Luce? *Nobody* called her that *ever!* She took another bottle from the chiller. She had bought two bottles but this was now the fifth, and she would have to replace them before anyone noticed they were gone. She really wasn't enjoying the evening anymore.

'Here goes, ladies,' she announced merrily, but truth was she was getting exhausted with the acting now. 'I'm afraid I'm going to have to make that the last one though as I have a really early start in the morning, as much as I'd love to carry on all night,' she said in mock disappointment.

'Lucy.'

The little voice coming from behind her confused her for a moment, being unexpected. The girls were now all looking in the direction of the door at little Lewis, who looked back at their drunk faces with a nervous smile. He was holding a tissue to his nose.

'Lewis,' she said a lot more calmly than she felt. He was supposed to stay in his room, they had a deal! 'What are you doing up?'

'I've got a nosebleed.' He tipped the tissue forward to show the blood he had collected.

'Oh dear,' she said kindly, ushering him out hurriedly. 'I'll be back in a minute.'

She was so grateful she had laid down the nephew story so that she didn't have to explain, but she just hoped that Lewis wouldn't mention her guests to his parents. *Oh well*, she thought, trying to stop herself from overreacting, *I am sure they wouldn't mind if I said they just popped in for ten minutes.*

'Let's sort you out.' She had a real soft spot for the little boy and couldn't be annoyed with him for coming down, he wasn't responsible for her mess. In fact, he had given her another reason to get them out of here.

'I'm really sorry, ladies, but I'm going to have to wrap things up, the poor boy's not feeling too good now and I'm going to have to settle him down.' She wondered if they were buying her fake disappointment, but she realised that actually she didn't care. She needed this friendship, or whatever it was, to end now, so she couldn't be too nice. 'Shall I call you a cab?'

'Yes please,' Kate said sensibly.

'Just one more bottle for the road,' slurred Natasha.

'I'm afraid not,' said Lucy, not apologising. She looked at Natasha and wondered why she had cared so much what she thought; she was nothing special, just a sad bully who had never grown up.

'Goodnight,' she called from the door as the taxi drove off, before running back indoors to restore order before Mr Kennedy came home.

# Chapter 47

Miami had been just what the doctor had ordered, and Susan Harrison had the spring back in her step when she came down to check out the next day. *Mario, Mario, Mario*, she thought dreamily, remembering the night before in every dreamy detail. It would keep her going for quite some time.

'Did you have a nice trip?' Sheena's voice interrupted her thoughts, and she realised she had managed to arrive in the hotel lobby from her room without taking any notice of the journey whatsoever, so caught up she was with her reminiscences.

'Oh yes, lovely thanks.' She couldn't contain the broad smile that was spread across her face. 'You?'

'Yes, it was really nice,' she smiled, looking over her shoulder to where Ray stood with the other pilots. To any of the other crew they were just casual work acquaintances, only Susan knowing different. Ray looked back at them both before quickly returning to his manly conversation with the captain. Susan knew he recognised her, for all she knew he recognised other girls on the crew too for the same reasons. It was easy for crew though, she had seen it many times before, to just act like nothing had happened in front of the others, nothing but a passing glance of mutual understanding between the perpetrators.

'I've changed your position on the way home, I've put you up the front, do you mind?'

'No of course not, is there an aircraft change?' That was usually the only reason why their positions would be changed.

'No, same aircraft.' She stepped closer to Susan and lowered her voice. 'One of the girls was just really getting on my nerves on the way out, flirting with Ray, and without telling her about us I can't say anything. I just don't know if I can bite my tongue so well on a night flight!'

'Oh.' Susan understood Sheena's reasoning, but the irony wasn't lost on her. She knew that Ray would never say anything about their night together though, and she was well practised at pretending nothing had happened. 'No problem.'

The flight was easy, a few more passengers than the way out but still less than half full, and they fell asleep quickly once they were fed. She would have been naive to have thought she could avoid Ray all flight, and when he walked into the galley to make a coffee, she couldn't help but be amused by the awkward look on his face.

'Hi, Ray,' she said cheerfully, knowingly, teasing him.

'Oh hi, how are you?' He, however, looked worried, and she knew he was wondering whether he was about to be outed, she could practically feel his nervousness.

'Good, thanks.' She was looking directly at him, but he

was looking anywhere except at her. Sheena was on her break, and obviously in the crew bunks this time, not the pilots'! 'So, did you have a nice trip?'

'Yeah, yeah, just a quiet one.' He was holding his cup under the coffee machine, poised ready to run out the minute it finished.

'Yes, Sheena said you had a nice time.' She knew she was being unkind but it was amusing her too much to stop.

'Ah, yes.' He turned to look at her quickly, probably trying to read her facial expression, his own face almost crimson now. The coffee machine gurgled to a halt. 'Right, anyway, I'd better get back, nice to see you again.'

And he was gone. Susan shook her head, laughing at how scared he seemed. He was somewhat less attractive to her now, seeing his less confident side; if you were going to sleep around, at least hold your head up high, like Susan Harrison did!


Susan Kennedy emptied the mail box on her way through the gates, the usual collection of brown and white envelopes, interspersed with fast food flyers. It was nearly midday and she couldn't decide whether it was worth even trying to have a nap before school pick up, or whether just to power through to an early night. She could always ask Lucy to pick the kids up, but she liked to do it herself when she had been away, and she felt surprisingly awake so she would probably do the latter.

It was cold, December was nearly upon them, and Susan's thoughts turned to Christmas decorations as she walked quickly into the house. She left her bag in the hall, going into the kitchen and putting the mail on the side. A phone beeped, and she was surprised to see Jeff's on the side, he had obviously forgotten it, which was very unlike him. She looked at the message that had flashed up on the screen;

*Just to confirm your reservation on 16th December for 14 people at 7pm for Christmas menu. We look forward to seeing you. Kind regards The Vestry Team*

Oh, that was something to look forward to, a Christmas party. She tried to remember if Jeff had mentioned anything before, he probably had but she had a terrible memory if anything was said on landing day, especially after champagne. With that many people there was bound to be a couple that she could have fun with, and besides she always enjoyed getting dressed up for a night in the city.

'Lucy, can I book you in for babysitting on the 16th?' Lucy had just walked into the room.

'Of course, and welcome back.'

'Thanks,' she said, picking up her own phone to call Jeff's office.

'Hi, Janice, can you please let Jeff know that he's left his phone at home, and that he has had a message to confirm the Christmas party.'

'Certainly.'

The unbroken tone told her that Janice had hung up, and she couldn't help looking at her phone, mouth agape. Even for Janice that was a bit rude, what had she ever done to upset her that much? Perhaps it wasn't such a good idea to go to the Christmas party after all, she wondered, before feeling the indignation rise. Why the hell shouldn't she go? Why should the sour-faced bitch make *her* feel uncomfortable? No, she was going. Oh yes, she was *definitely* going!

# Chapter 48

'Hello, darling, how was your flight?' Jeff arrived home just after the kids had gone to bed, and Susan was half of the way down a bottle of champagne, trying to stay awake.

'Good, thanks,' she answered without thinking; she could hardly tell him all about it so a standard answer would do in this case, as usual.

'Ah, my phone.' Jeff looked pleased to be reunited with it as Susan handed it to him. 'I was hoping I'd left it here and not on the train or something. Thanks for letting me know.'

'There was a message on it about the Christmas party, I did ask Janice to tell you. I'm really looking forward to it,' she said brightly.

'Oh, oh yes,' he stammered. 'I meant to mention that to you!' He seemed awkward, as if he needed to dig himself out of a hole. It made her wonder if perhaps he hadn't forgotten at all, if he had chosen not to mention it. 'I've only just booked it, it's not a party really, just a bite to eat for the guys at the office. It might be a bit boring for you, if you'd rather not come I'd completely understand.'

'No,' she protested. 'I'd love to come, you haven't had a Christmas party for years.'

In the early days she had known everyone at Jeff's work but since the children had come along she rarely got in to the office, and it would be nice to be able to put some faces to names.

'Great, well let's hope Lucy can babysit.'

'Done,' she said affirmatively.

'Oh well, you have it all sorted then. Great,' he said again. 'I had better book an extra seat.'

It was probably just the tiredness but she thought that she felt a reluctance in his voice and wondered if he even wanted her to go, if he had never intended to invite her. She felt an unfamiliar feeling of insecurity, but she tried to brush it off, telling herself that she was jumping to the wrong conclusions.

'Do you mind me coming?' she asked childishly, unable to control her emotions.

'Of course I don't, I'd love you to come, I just didn't think a lot of work talk would be your thing.' He had obviously seen the hurt look on her face, and he put his arms around her.

'I'm sure I can hold my own,' she assured him. Had he forgotten that she was an international flight attendant who could make conversation with just about anyone, in any situation? Even the most boring of his friends?

'Yes, I know you can.' He kissed the top of her head and exhaled inexplicably as he released his hold of her. She was definitely being oversensitive, reading too much into things, this was Jeff, the man who loved her to the moon and back, and would want her with him everywhere he went, wouldn't he?

She sat back down at the island and watched her husband as he caught up with his estranged phone, sipping her champagne. Susan Harrison was silent now that she had been satisfied, and Susan Kennedy was grateful for all that she had, all that he gave her, for the security, *because that was a given.*

'I'm going up, don't be long,' she announced as she got down from her seat, winking theatrically at him. She thought how cute he looked when he smiled back at her, creases ever deeper around his eyes.

'I've just got a couple of emails to send and I'll be up,' he said, clearly amused by her comedic innuendo.

The champagne helped her to float up the stairs and into her room. Despite always staying in nice hotels there was no bed more inviting than her own. Lucy would always put on fresh sheets on landing day, and it was made beautifully with all of its cushions and throws.

She practically skipped over to the dressing table, sitting down as she took out her hair, placing the pins back into the small drawer where they would stay until her next flight. She opened her drawer of makeup, a quick freshen up to look her best, and rummaged around for her old highlighter that always seemed to give her that natural glow in the bedroom lighting.

*That's strange*, she thought, several minutes later when she was unable to find it. As she looked further into the drawer she was sure that it was emptier, that other things were perhaps missing too, not that she could put her finger on exactly what right now. Sophia was reaching that age, she guessed, 'borrowing' things. She would have to have it out with her in the morning, lay down some rules along the lines of asking before you take things!

She reached out for the perfume which she knew Jeff liked best, and sprayed herself liberally. As she put it back down she noticed that that too was looking emptier; surely it was a little heavy for a twelve-year-old, she thought, she couldn't imagine her daughter choosing that particular fragrance? Oh well, she sighed, she was sure that she wasn't the only mother of a preteen to be missing some things, and none of it was important, she just *really* liked that highlighter!

'Just tell me the truth, Sophia, it's no big deal, I just want my highlighter back.' Susan was frustrated, she hadn't expected it to get this serious. She thought she would just mention it and Sophia would simply apologise and give her back the highlighter, it didn't need to be an argument; but here they were, in the kitchen, and Sophia was visibly upset.

'I promise, Mum, I haven't taken anything from your room, I haven't even been in there while you've been away.'

Her daughter's big round eyes were glazed with tears and Susan believed her, she knew her well enough to know when she was lying.

'Well then it must have been you, Lewis.' She looked at her son, trying to lighten the situation. It was only an old highlighter after all, not worth tears.

'Hey?' He looked up from his iPad.

She tried to keep a straight face as her sweet boy looked at her in confused innocence.

'Have you been using my makeup whilst I was away, huh?'

'No!' The poor thing looked shocked at the accusation, and Susan couldn't hold her laughter back, pleased to see that it had the same effect on Sophia.

'Oh, I'm sorry, darling, I was only teasing.' She leant over and hugged him, before moving over to hug her daughter. 'And I'm sorry if I upset you, I didn't mean to. I must have misplaced it.'

'Excuse me,' Lucy interrupted, trying to get past her with the mop and bucket.

'Oh, sorry, Lucy.' Susan hadn't even noticed that she was there, and she moved to let her by. 'Oh, Lucy, I was thinking to get the Christmas decorations down this weekend, would you mind helping me to put them up next week?'

'Of course,' Lucy said, without looking back, obviously not in a very talkative mood.

'Yay,' cheered Sophia, eyes dry now, subject changed. Susan loved Christmas and this was going to be a great one.

# Chapter 49

It was December 1st, and in Susan Kennedy's house that meant one thing... Christmas had started! The same music that played every year was pulsating over the speakers that were connected wirelessly around the house, and the dozen or so boxes of decorations were sitting in the hall greeting her when she came back from dropping the kids at school.

'I'm back, Lucy,' she called, needing her help to tackle the job in hand. Lucy appeared within moments, knowing exactly how this all went, taking the box marked 'Lounge', and walking off in that direction without saying a word. Susan remembered previous years when she and Lucy had had lovely times putting up the decorations, but things seemed different this year, and she didn't know why. To be honest, it was one of those problems that you hoped would just sort themselves out, that you were too busy to think about despite its constant niggling. Like it wasn't important enough in your own life to dedicate your *own* energy to, and heaven forbid have to solve it. But Lucy hadn't been right since her mum died. Sometimes she was better than others, but it had been months, and quite frankly her lack of enthusiasm and general misery was starting to get to Susan.

Susan caught herself, shocked at her own derision. Lucy had been a wonderful employee, and at times almost counted as a friend. Perhaps she should have been less self-centred and actually reached out to her, tried to help. It was clear she wasn't herself, going through the motions and doing her job as effectively as always, but just in silence. Maybe *she* needed a friend? Susan needed to do something to help, she wasn't sure what, but she would have a good think, right after she had finished with this.

Susan sang merrily along to The Pogues as she fixed the garlands to the spindles on the staircase. She was relieved at Jeff's foresight one year to get invisible fixings that just remained up year-round, making this job much easier. Standing back and admiring her work a short time later she felt almost giddy with excitement, it was the highest she had felt without champagne for a long time. Christmases weren't particularly great memories from her own childhood, and hence since she had her own family she had thrown everything into making sure that theirs were their happiest.

'Lucy, come and see this.' She needed to share with somebody her utter joy at the way the hall was looking, hoping to extract some happiness at the same time.

'Very nice,' said Lucy, poking her head around the door without an ounce of enthusiasm, before disappearing again. Susan tried not to let it ruin her own happiness, pushing back against the anger that was threatening;

enough was enough now!

*No*, she chided herself. Now was not the time for anger, Lucy was obviously depressed.

But it was ruining her enjoyment of putting up the decorations, *she* was ruining it.

Susan recognised her inner sulking schoolgirl and took a deep breath, exhaling her from her body. Just because she was happy and looking forward to Christmas, maybe Lucy wasn't, maybe Lucy hated the whole idea now that her mum wasn't here. Oh hell, she had been so selfish and thoughtless! Of course! Of course Lucy was going to be miserable, the poor thing, *her* Christmas was going to be a time of sadness.

Susan stood motionless, the noise of the music fading out. When had she become so out of touch? When had she become so self-centred that she didn't even see what was going on around her, with those that were always there for her?

'Lucy?' she said softly, walking into the lounge.

Lucy was at the far end putting some lights around the mirror.

'Yes?'

'I'm really sorry if I've been insensitive.'

Lucy hesitated for a moment, fixing the last strand of fairy lights before turning around. Her head was cocked, face confused, she obviously had no idea what Susan was referring to.

'Look, I know you must be dreading Christmas, what with your mum passing, and I'm sorry that I've forced you into doing all of this.' She gestured around at the decorations.

Lucy still looked confused, as if she hadn't actually

considered the connection herself.

'Oh, it's fine, honestly, whatever you need me to do.'

'No, it's not fine, Lucy, I hadn't even given it a thought that you might not be looking forward to Christmas yourself.'

'Honestly, I'm okay, you don't need to worry about me.' Lucy was managing a small smile. It was a kind, grateful smile that made Susan feel even worse.

'What are your plans for Christmas?' Susan asked.

'Oh, I don't know yet, it's still weeks away.'

'Well you're always welcome to spend it with us.'

'Oh, do you need help?'

'No!' Susan was shocked that she thought she was that shallow. 'No, I mean as a friend, not an employee!'

'Oh.' She looked as if she really didn't know how to receive the offer. 'That's very kind of you, but I will probably be with family.'

'Well that's okay then,' Susan said, pleased that she had some sort of plan, 'but the offer is always there, Lucy. You're not just an employee, we count you as a friend, you know.'

Susan was aware that Lucy was looking a bit uneasy, obviously uncomfortable with the blurred lines of this relationship, and decided to end the pep talk.

'Anyway, I just need you to know that I'm here if you want to talk, and if you can't bear the thought of Christmas please just take the rest of today off. I'm sorry that in my own excitement I forgot that it might be a difficult time for you.'

Lucy was still standing motionless, staring back at her, saying nothing.

'Right, anyway, I'm off to do my room,' Susan muttered, sensing it was time to leave poor Lucy alone. She found the box marked 'master bedroom,' climbing the stairs two at a time to get there. She had done the right thing, been sympathetic, but now she needed to get her Christmas spirit back.


Sophia and Lewis squealed in delight when they saw the finished result after school. It had taken her all day but Susan was pleased with her work, no room left untouched by the festive spirit.

'When's the tree coming?' Lewis asked.

Right on cue the doorbell rang, and Susan couldn't hold back the smile as she opened it to reveal Luke, dragging a huge pine tree behind him.

'Awwwesoome,' declared Sophia. Even wrapped in its net they could see that it was even bigger than last year's.

'Right, come on then, let's help him get it in,' ordered Susan, the children rushing past Luke to 'help' carry it.

'Hello, aunty,' Luke called as Lucy was walking past them busily, but she ignored him, something that wasn't lost on Susan. She looked at Luke, who just shrugged his shoulders, as if he too was at a loss with her.

They heaved the tree into position in the lounge, standing it in the bracket that Susan had placed there earlier. Luke stood back as his job was done, looking pleased with his work.

'Can we start putting the decorations on, Mum?' asked Sophia.

'No, honey, you know we always wait for Daddy to do that,' she said kindly. 'But you can make a start on your rooms!'

Two boxes still sat in the hall, labelled 'Sophia' and

'Lewis.' They held the eclectic mix of decorations that they had acquired over their few years. The cuddly toys that danced, the glittery pine cones they had decorated at preschool, and a whole host of random things that she was happy for them to put up, in their own rooms, where it didn't matter about coordination! Of course, there were a few special things that they had made that would be making it onto the tree again this year, like every other year, just not *everything*.

'Come on, Lewis, let's see who finishes their room first,' challenged Sophia.

She watched them eagerly climb the stairs with their boxes, forgetting that there was anyone else in the world at the moment, until she turned to see Luke was smiling at her. She smiled back, in a contented motherly way, not in the way that Susan Harrison had once smiled at him.

# Chapter 50

'Oh, Sophia, it looks beautiful,' Susan said, looking around her daughter's room, having just been called up for the big reveal.

'Mum, now come and see mine,' Lewis said impatiently, taking her hand and pulling her in the direction of his room.

'Wow, Lewis, it looks amazing,' she gushed convincingly, looking around at his haphazard decorating. Tinsel hung from everything, and the cuddly toys that had long since lost their ability to sing and dance were lined up across the centre of the room as if off to battle. It was a far cry from Sophia's carefully draped lights and pretty things, all coordinated and girly.

'So, whose is best?' His broad smile said that he thought his room was definitely the winner, despite the smugness of his sister, who was standing in his doorway looking around with a definite sneer on her face.

'Oh, darling, they are both wonderful, I couldn't possibly choose.' Susan hated it when they insisted that she choose a winner, she couldn't bear the disappointment of the one who lost. Ultimately Sophia, being the eldest, was generally the better drawer, runner, decorator, and so on, which explained her eagerness to make everything a competition, but Lewis was still young and naive enough to believe he was a strong contender in everything.

'Muuum.' Sophia was annoyed. 'I hate it when you do that, just choose.'

Susan looked at her daughter, wishing she could for a brief moment go back a couple of years, to when she couldn't do anything wrong in her eyes.

'Sophia, I'm sorry, but they are just two completely different styles, so I can't compare them.' Susan was pleased with her answer, logging it for use in future similar situations. Sophia just rolled her eyes. No doubt in another year or two she would need to up her game even more, but for now she had won the battle.

'Anyway,' she added, looking at her watch, 'Dad will be home soon to do the tree, so I'm just going to go and freshen up.' She had been working hard all day and didn't want to look quite so dishevelled when her husband arrived home.

She walked into her room, sat down at her dressing table, and stared at the face that looked back at her from the mirror. It was looking a little tired, she thought, or maybe age was finally catching up with her, but nothing a little makeup wouldn't sort out. Opening her drawer, she took out her bag of everyday miracles, the things that she couldn't do without. Just as she went to close it something caught her eye and she stopped in her tracks. The highlighter that had been missing was looking back at her, as if it had never been gone. In fact, the drawer seemed to be fuller again, although she had never really worked out what else had been taken. She wondered for a moment if Sophia had snuck it back, but then remembered the tears and how she had believed her daughter that day. No, she must have just missed it, and the drawer had always been this full, she shrugged, not entirely convinced.

The thunder of the kids' footsteps down the stairs and excited voices heralded Jeff's return. Susan looked down from the landing at the happy scene and descended quickly to join in the group hug. She loved that Jeff was always as excited as her to start the Christmas celebrations, and decorating the tree together on the first of December was their family tradition.


'Let me just take my coat off,' he laughed as the children pulled him into the lounge. 'Wow, would you look at the size of that!' he declared, stopping in his tracks and looking up at the tree, awestruck.

Susan was pleased at his reaction. Luke had excelled this year in his task to get the best tree yet.

'Let me take that,' she said as she took his coat off him. 'The lights are just there, all tested and ready for you.'

'Well I'd better get stuck in then,' he said, clearly aware that two pairs of young eyes were sitting watching him intently, waiting for him to light this big boy up. Susan returned minutes later as Jeff was leaning precariously from the stepladder putting the last of the bulbs at the top of the tree.

'Right, hit the switch,' he called down, and both of the children scrabbled for the socket.

'Careful, you two,' Susan warned.

The lights transformed the green pine into a beautiful

centrepiece, and they were all silent for a moment as they admired it.

'Well that's that,' said Jeff, now at the foot of the ladder.

'Can we start now?' asked Lewis, breaking the silence.

'Of course,' said Susan.

Two huge boxes of decorations sat on the floor, enough baubles for each branch to wear one, she was sure. She would let them all do their worst, carefree and oblivious of her desire of uniform spacing and symmetry. Then later, when they went to bed she would work her magic, a few changes here and there and all would be well.

'Ooh,' cooed Sophia at the big chiffon bows that Susan had brought back recently from the States.

'Aren't they beautiful,' Susan beamed, remembering all of the trees in the hotel lobbies that she had seen wearing them, hoping that this tree would be just as beautiful, eventually.

Jeff's arm felt nice around her shoulder as they stood and watched their offspring work together, without arguments, on their project.

'Don't you just love Christmas,' Susan said excitedly, looking up at him.

'You know I do.' Jeff leant down and kissed her.

The moment was perfect, everything about it, until…

'Oh, I've been meaning to mention it, but Mum and Dad were hoping to come for Christmas this year, to stay a couple of days. They want to enjoy it with the family.'

Susan felt her body tense, and she didn't care if Jeff felt it too, he wasn't so stupid as not to know this would never be well received.

'But they always go on their cruise,' Susan said lamely, trying to hide her despair.

'I know.' Jeff at least had the decency to sound unhappy about it too. 'Look, I know they can be difficult, but they're getting old, and I couldn't say no.'

Susan looked up at him. So that was that, the decision had been made and since she had no control over the situation she could only control how she dealt with it now. Maybe he did have a point, she reasoned reluctantly, they *were* old, but she didn't know if she could hold it together if they ruined her Christmas. It had always just been them on Christmas Day, with family visits around the holiday, but the day was always just *theirs*. She would have loved to have had the big family feasts that she had seen in pictures, but what with her often difficult family, and his, she had always been happy for it to be just them. The fact that his parents always went on a cruise had just made it easier for it to be that way.

'It will be fine,' she said eventually, once she had convinced herself, and she could sense the imaginary weight lift off his shoulders.

'Thank you, I do love you.' He held her tight for a moment.

Susan looked around her when he let her go, at all that he gave her. How could she be difficult over his parents coming for Christmas? No, they wouldn't spoil it, it would be as wonderful as always.

# Chapter 51

Lucy sank into the worn armchair and put her head in her hands. Today had been such a hard day, to be surrounded by all of the Kennedys' Christmas cheer while she would have loved to have pretended that the whole season wasn't even happening. She had been on autopilot all day, trying to go through the motions, treating it all as just a job that needed doing. She had even managed to block out the music that Mrs Kennedy had insisted on playing, listening to her own, more sombre soundtrack in her head instead.

She hadn't really been thinking about her mum, although it was always there, and when Mrs Kennedy had brought it all up she had been thrown for a moment. No, she had been thinking about lots of other things, the whole pile of problems that were stacked on her shoulders. Well, at least her mum's passing was obviously excusing her from having to act at being okay, because she wasn't okay, not at all.

She looked despairingly at the pile of envelopes that sat on the mantelpiece. The ones at the bottom were open, but not the top ones. She had stopped opening them a while ago, when she realised she couldn't afford to pay them anymore, the credit card bills that had somehow got so out of control.

She thought back to where it had all started, trying to work out where she had lost control. She had never had a credit card before, but when Mum had died, she hadn't wanted to admit to her family that she couldn't afford to help with the funeral, she didn't want them to know that she was poor. It wasn't that the Kennedys paid her badly, not at all, but whatever money that she had spare had gone to feed her gambling habit. It was only harmless fun, sometimes she would win and sometimes she would lose, but she never spent more than she had, so why should she feel guilty about it? She would stay up late at night trying to outwit the computers that would almost always win, for those rare moments of euphoria when *she* would be the winner. Some people drank, some smoked, some partied or bought expensive clothes, so why shouldn't she spend her money on something that she enjoyed?

Anyhow, without any savings she had succumbed to the lure of the credit card and the bills that were piling up were a testament to her weakness. First a casket, and yes her mum would have the best, she could pay it off in her own time. Then the wake, they had all just wanted a few sandwiches in the local boozer, but Lucy had seen how things were done properly, at the Kennedys', and she wanted *that* for her mum. She may not have been able to do it for her when she was alive, but she knew her mum would have loved to have seen the people she cared about appreciating the catering as they sat in the upmarket golf club, commenting on how well her daughter had done.

Until then she had thought it was under control, even working out how much she would need to pay each month to get it paid off, incorporating it into her bills. But it kept going up, not down, mostly spurred on by her new fake friends, and having to keep up appearances. The new shoes, the champagne and food. Now they were inviting her out for dinners, and she was having to buy clothes, she couldn't risk borrowing Mrs Kennedy's anymore, not after she had noticed the makeup missing, and the sleepless nights she had had until she had managed to sneak it all back. Now she would have to spend a small fortune on makeup too, she couldn't go back to the cheap stuff she had been satisfied with before all of this.

Her phone pinged and she lifted it up reluctantly.

'Are you home tomorrow for a coffee?'

It was Kate. Lucy wailed quietly, looking upward, as if maybe only a higher being could help her now.

'No, sorry, I have lots of errands to run this week, Christmas shopping!' she replied, lying, wondering when all of the lies were going to implode on her, because they were certain to one day.

'No worries, let me know when you are free.'

'Will do.' Lucy was grateful for Kate's easy-going manner; maybe she would suggest meeting somewhere next week. She had to admit she actually enjoyed Kate's company, although she wished she didn't have to keep up her own lies whilst Kate gave her all her truths. She would have to dissolve the friendship soon, there really wasn't any other option, but she was just waiting for it to happen naturally, reluctant to engineer it. A small part of her thought that Kate might even forgive her if she explained how it had all happened, but her sensible side knew that she wouldn't really want to be her friend anymore, and that she would tell the others. That was what she was scared of, the ridicule and scorn of Natasha and her peers. They would have an absolute field day, and she didn't think that she could handle it any better now than she had as that insecure schoolgirl.

A knock on the door was a welcome relief from her thoughts, not that she was expecting anyone. A sudden panic gripped her; what if Natasha had found out about her and come here to 'out' her? She stood motionless for a minute, grappling with reality, before walking as silently as she could along the hall.

'It's me, Luke,' called the familiar voice of her nephew. She forgot for a moment that she was not talking to him, such was her relief that it was only him. She opened the door, replacing her relieved face with a stern one.

'What are you doing here?' she asked coldly.

'I came to see if you are okay?' He was looking at her so sweetly she felt the anger with him waning.

'I'm fine, thank you.'

'No, you're not, aunty,' he said in a kind but firm voice. 'Let me in, I need to talk to you.'


'Let me make us a cuppa,' Luke said, walking through to her kitchen. He knew her too well, and she was struggling to stay mad with him. 'Then you can tell me what I have done wrong. I'm not putting up with you ignoring me anymore!' He gave her a cheeky smile, the one that had won her over so many times when he was a little boy. Without her own children Lucy had had plenty of time and energy to devote to being an aunty, and Luke had always been her favourite. Perhaps that was why she had been so upset with his behaviour, so disappointed. She sat back in her armchair and waited for him to bring in the tea, going over what she would say.

'Here you go.' He handed her a mug and sat down on the sofa, leaning forward. 'Now hit me with it, what have I done?'

'Oh, Luke,' she said sadly, looking down at the tea, 'how could you do it? You've got a lovely girlfriend, and that beautiful baby, and yet you're sleeping around with these rich women who don't even care about you.' Her anger had turned to disappointment and she had tears in her eyes as she looked up at him.

'Oh.' It was Luke's turn now to look down at his tea. He was silent for a while, and she was relieved that he didn't try to deny it. 'I'm sorry, aunty, I don't know why I do it, it's just hard to say no.'

She nodded. She wasn't stupid, or naive. Luke was a good-looking young man and she doubted that many men like him would be able to say no if the likes of Mrs Kennedy threw themselves at them. She respected him a little more now though, if only for his honesty, glad that he was still close enough to her to open up.

'But, Luke, aren't you happy? Is it worth risking every-thing you have for a leg-over in the summer house?'

Luke's eyes opened wider; he was obviously startled by her true understanding of the situation. He nodded his head, and she could see that he knew she was right.

'It's all over now anyway,' he said eventually, confirm-ing what she had suspected for a while anyway.

'I hope so, Luke, that they are *all* over.' Oh yes, he had to know that she knew there was more than one. 'If I can find out about others, Luke, then so can anybody.' She wasn't going to go into how she found out, then he would be able to judge *her,* and right now this was about him.

'Point taken, I know I've been stupid,' he said. He sounded earnest enough, but she wondered if he would be able to resist any future temptation. At least she wouldn't have to know about it anymore though if it was over with Mrs Kennedy, and she did believe him on that.

'So now that that's all out in the open, can you stop ignoring me now please, I've been missing my favourite aunt,' he grinned.

She couldn't help but smile back. It felt good to smile, she hadn't done that for some time. As she hugged him goodbye an hour later she clung on for just a moment longer than she normally would.

'Are you sure you're okay?' Luke pulled back and looked at her seriously.

'I will be,' she said as a tear rolled down her cheek and he hugged her again.

'You know where I am, just call me if you need anything, okay?'

She nodded and closed the door behind him. Despite all of her new 'friends', Lucy felt lonelier now than she ever had done, alone with her troubles. She looked at the pile of letters again, picking them up and taking them to the armchair with her. She had just sat there and told Luke to sort himself out, now she was telling herself. She didn't have a mother to scold her, or an aunt to tell her off; she was a grown woman now, and had to sort out her own problems. As she opened the envelopes she took a deep breath. Nothing would be solved by burying her head in the sand, she would have to do something, about the money *and* the 'friends'. She needed to get back to her old self, in her old life, where she didn't feel lonely and out of control.

# Chapter 52

Susan took one last look at the long list, having just ticked off the 'M&S food order', closing her notebook and dropping it onto her bag. Christmas was only two weeks away and she didn't feel as prepared as she usually did. It was probably because Jeff's parents were coming, the extra pressure of his mum's critical eye taking some of her usual enjoyment out of it. She was nearly there though, and a few hours in the shopping mall in Toronto would hopefully be enough to finish off. She could be going absolutely anywhere in the world with the amount of sightseeing that she would be doing this trip. As much as she loved the Canadian city it was firstly too cold in the winter for her to go outside, and secondly it had an amazing mall near their hotel where she could happily get lost for hours.

'Bye, Lucy, thanks for everything,' she called as she opened the front door. Jeff was at work and Lucy would be picking the kids up from school in a few hours. Susan stopped for a moment to do up her coat, to protect her against the wind that howled across the driveway. She hoped that she had used enough hairspray to hold her style in this weather.

'Oh, you're welcome. Have a safe flight.' Lucy came out from the kitchen, drying her hands on a tea towel. She definitely seemed a bit brighter now, Susan thought, relieved, hoping that she had turned a corner.

She lifted her near-empty suitcase into the boot of her Range Rover, along with her small cabin bag. They would both be bursting on the way home, if previous Christmas shopping trips were anything to go by. Looking back at the house as she got into the driver's side, she smiled at the lit-up reindeer that stood around the lawn, and the endless lights that hung from the roof, still glowing in the darkness of the winter's day. Susan Kennedy was a lucky lady, and she would have to keep that in mind if Christmas became at all difficult!

As many times as she had done it, there was absolutely *nothing* that Susan enjoyed about doing a manual demonstration. She walked reluctantly to her demo position, carrying her beige leather pouch, dropping it unceremoniously on the floor at the aircraft door.

'It will be good for you all to have a little refresher,' the flight manager had smiled in the briefing, taking it upon herself to give them all the opportunity. Most managers were quite happy just to play the video and get the crew to point out the exits, but oh no, not Martha Blakeman, the smiling assassin! *How to get a flight off to a good start, piss off your crew*, Susan thought, looking up the aircraft at Martha as she sat smugly on her jump seat watching them.

'A copy of the safety instruction card is in your seat pocket.' Martha's raspy voice rattled over the PA. Susan held up the laminated card, struggling to keep the faint smile on her face as she turned it around. Susan Harrison wouldn't have struggled quite so much, but once again Susan Kennedy had come to work, all full of family and Christmas, and not needing to be here, it definitely wasn't the right job for this Susan.

'A life jacket is underneath your seat....' Susan shook out the yellow rubber inflatable, getting it caught in her hair as she put it clumsily over her head. 'Blow in the tube like this...' Susan Harrison would have made this funny, but Susan Kennedy just pinched the small black tube between her fingers, letting it quickly go again. She hoped that she would never have to don a life jacket on an aircraft for real, for that would be a really bad day.

'Oxygen masks will fall from overhead....' *Oh, will this fun never end*, Susan cried silently, glad that it was nearly over. Sometimes nobody would watch you, but today the passengers were obviously not so well travelled, all watching her intently, heads sticking out in the aisles or over the tops of the seats in front of them.

'The cabin crew will point out your exits now....' It was the bit that everyone knew, and she saw at least three camera phones pointed at her as she extended her arms, turning around and pointing out the exits behind her. It crossed her mind for a minute that if any of those videos which had just been taken were to end up in the wrong hands she would actually be embarrassed, and for the first time ever she wondered if Jeff's mum might actually be right. She pictured the horsey mums in the playground laughing at her in her rubber jacket and felt her cheeks flush. Susan Harrison wouldn't have cared what they thought, but *she* wasn't here today, there was too much shopping to be done for *her* distractions.

'Thank God that's over,' Susan said back in the galley as she put her props back into their pouch.

'Oh, I know,' said Claire in agreement. Susan had flown with her before, but neither of them could recall where. 'I can't stand it either.'

That made Susan feel better, that it wasn't just a Susan Kennedy thing. She was a bit afraid lately, what with Susan Harrison's shrinking circle, that this may not be the job for her anymore, and that made her sad. After all, once upon a time she had enjoyed it without the excitement of the other men, and she hoped that she could find her love for it again as this Susan. She still had the lure of the lifestyle, the hotels, the shopping without distractions, the beaches, the nights out......what other job would give her all of that? She imagined herself just staying at home and realised that she did still need this, as a Harrison, or a Kennedy, and she was relieved. Yes, the haters could laugh at her if they wanted, but they wouldn't be shopping in Canada tomorrow, or ordering room service tonight.

'Are you coming for a drink tonight?' Claire asked as they sat on their jumpseats at the back doors as the plane taxied to the runway.

'Yes,' Susan said without hesitation. It hadn't been her original plan for the trip, but Susan Kennedy needed to find her love for it again, it wasn't *all* about Susan Harrison after all.

# Chapter 53

Wherever they were in the world the pilots could always sniff out an Irish bar, and that was exactly where they had found themselves. The usual dark wood floors and wall panelling, the picture of a shamrock above the door, along with the Irish bar staff, told you exactly where you were. It was happy hour too, of course, generally the deciding factor on which bar they went to, and the drinks were soon flowing to the long table that the crew were occupying. It was a good turnout, only a couple not coming, Martha thankfully being one of them.

This was one of the things that Susan, either one, did love, how a group of people who had probably never met before, could sit in a bar and make conversation about *anything*. From poached eggs to more risqué subjects as the drinks went down, nothing was ever off limits, and no language too colourful.

'How's Olivia, Claire?' Gemma, who had been working in the front cabin leant across and asked Claire, who was sitting next to Susan.

'Yeah, she's getting there, I think, they're trying to work

through things,' Claire replied in a serious tone.

'Who's that?' asked Susan, wondering who they were talking about.

'Olivia Kaye, do you know her?' Claire asked.

Susan shook her head slowly.

'I don't think I do, but the name rings a bell. What happened to her?' Susan was rubbish at remembering names, there had been far too many in this job. 'If you don't mind me asking?'

'Oh, I'm sure she won't mind me talking about it, she's quite open,' Claire shrugged. Susan doubted that it would have mattered if she did or didn't, as clearly Claire wasn't one for keeping confidences. 'Her fiancé was having an affair, and the crazy bitch he was sleeping with pretended to be pregnant with his baby, stalked her, and then nearly killed her.'

Claire said it with a matter-of-factness that came from telling the story many times. Susan was shocked, and sat for a while in stunned silence, trying to process all of the separate parts that she had just heard, especially the last bit.

'Tried to kill her?!' she exclaimed, eventually.

'Yep, right outside my house, she ran her over.' Claire held up her empty wine glass to signal the waitress over.

'Oh my God.' Susan was still shocked. 'What the hell was he thinking getting involved with someone crazy like that?' Susan suddenly flashed back to Mark and his wife, there were nutters everywhere she guessed.

'It was Olivia who introduced them ironically, offered her a job as his personal assistant, but she wanted her man too.' Claire shrugged again as the waitress appeared. 'A Chardonnay and nachos please.'

'Another white wine for me too please,' Susan added to the order. She tried to think of any comparisons that could be drawn from her own affairs but she was pretty sure that none of them were going to try and kill Jeff, the unlikelihood of it amusing her a little.

'So, watch your husbands' secretaries, girls,' warned Claire, looking around the table seriously before smiling to signal she was finished.

It hit Susan in the stomach, and caught her by absolute surprise, the image of Janice wanting Jeff, of her *actually* pursuing her husband. Was she stupid to honestly believe that he wouldn't be tempted? It wasn't the first time it had crossed her mind, but it was the first time it had made her feel like this, made her stomach flip.

'Thank you.' Her wine arrived just in time, and she took a big gulp in an effort to wash away the thoughts. 'So, are they still together?'

'Yep, but I think she's struggling to forget it all.'

'I bet,' Susan said. She had wondered on more than one occasion whether Jeff would forgive her if he ever found anything out, and now she wondered if she could ever forgive him, despite being fully aware that meant she had double standards.

'The shame was that Tom, her other half, was a really good guy, he just didn't have enough willpower to fight the girl off, she was too calculating for him.' Claire was still talking but Susan's mind was wandering now, remembering how gorgeous Janice had looked the last time she saw her, wondering if Jeff would be able to resist her if she decided to have him.

'I hope they can get through it,' she said, and she meant

it. She was sure Tom's affair had been as meaningless as all of hers, that he never meant to hurt their relationship any more than she wanted to risk hers. The only difference was that Jeff would never find out about Susan Harrison, she wasn't even his wife... oh but then there was Luke, but that was over now. Susan shook herself, this whole train of thought was pointless.

'Anyone for shots?' she said loudly, looking around the table for allies. She needed to get wasted now, after all of that, and by the show of hands she wasn't the only one!

Susan looked down at herself in the bed, fully clothed including her shoes. It had been a long time since she had woken up down route like this, and she let out a chuckle that was quickly silenced by the pain in her head. So, Susan had made it to bed, alone, despite the amount of alcohol that had clearly been drunk. Maybe it was okay to be Susan Kennedy at work, apparently *she* could have a pretty good time too!

She kicked off her heels and got up slowly, making her way to the bathroom, hoping that there were some painkillers in her wash bag. She still had a full day of shopping to get through, and a night flight home, so this current state of disability just wouldn't do!

# Chapter 54

'*Susan!*' Susan had been a million miles away until Martha's voice brought her back to reality.

'I'm sorry, what was the question?' She didn't care that the manager was looking at her as if she wanted to kill her, who did a full inbound safety briefing anyway? It was completely unnecessary, and in her current state of weakness from both the hangover and the shopping, she could really do without it.

'How do you deploy a raft and separate it?' Martha said sternly, looking at her like a Victorian schoolteacher. Susan stopped herself from groaning and rolling her eyes like a naughty schoolchild in response.

'Open the door in automatic......' she recited the procedure that was drilled into them every year on their safety training. It was another in the long list of things that she knew which she hoped she would never have to put into practice. Riding the waves of the North Atlantic in an inflatable raft with sixty people in it, trying to tie up to the others, set off flares and scare off sharks, all while administering first aid, repairing punctures and collecting rainwater just didn't sound like something she could easily do. It was a nice idea of course, that they had a backup plan if things went *really* wrong, but she would much rather be inside the plane giving out meals than doing all of that!

Relieved that the briefing was over they all returned to their parts of the plane to get ready for boarding. Susan joined the queue for the crew cart; even a dry tuna sandwich would be welcome right now, anything to mop up this upset stomach. How she had got through the day's shopping she had no idea, but she had, and now her list was all ticked off, and as predicted her cases were bursting at the seams.

'Whose idea were the shots?' groaned Gemma.

'Sorry, mine,' Susan said apologetically. She was grateful that she wasn't the only one suffering.

'PA check from the flight deck.' They all stopped talking as the captain made his announcement. 'Eight and a half hours home tonight. There's a lot of weather around so I will be keeping you all strapped in for a while after take-off. Here comes the evac alarm test.' Horns started beeping from the doors and the crew scattered to go and turn them off, giving Martha a thumbs up to confirm they were working.

As Susan sat at her door thirty minutes later, the captain's words came back to her. 'Some weather,' he had said. The connotations of what he had said had missed her, but now as their aircraft struggled through the invisible hills and mountains of the air, she wished that she had paid more attention, been more mentally prepared. Her stomach reeled as she was reduced to near-weightlessness for a moment, before being pulled heavily back into her seat again.

The engines sounded as if they were straining to climb this mountain, and the noise of the hydraulics seemed much louder than normal as the pilots adjusted every flap they had to negotiate the climb. It seemed to go on forever and Susan could feel the watery sensation at the back of her mouth that warned her the tuna sandwich might not be staying down much longer. Against all safety protocol she released herself from her straps and, clinging to the handle that was moulded into the wall behind her, reached into the small galley cupboard that held the sick bags.... just in time!

Claire looked across at her in amused sympathy.

'Oh, babe, are you okay?'

'Better now, thanks,' Susan replied, sure that she had nothing left to bring up. She was relieved that the plane seemed to have climbed above the weather now and things were starting to settle.

'Excuse me,' a voice called from just in front of the galley. Susan glanced out to see a lady holding her own sick bag in the aisle. Susan looked at it, and then down at her own, which she was still holding.

'One moment.' She opened the canister holding the first aid kit and located the big yellow bags. The seatbelt signs pinged off and she walked into the aisle to relieve her fellow sick lady of her own stomach contents.

'Excuse me' another call from further up, and another sick bag.

Five minutes later Susan had completed her lap of the cabin and returned to the galley with her bag full of vomit from at least twenty stomachs. Her colleagues had watched her from the galley, laughing uncontrollably at her tortured face, and could barely speak as she walked past them.

'That,' she said, looking at the bag that she had dropped unceremoniously on the floor, 'was the *worst* thing I have ever had to do on a hangover.'

Gemma gave her a hug, and Susan could feel the shakes of her laughter, having to concede and find the funny side too. She was relieved to notice that strangely her hangover had lifted, deciding that it must now be at the bottom of the yellow bag.


Susan enjoyed the euphoria that you get when you finally feel better, suddenly becoming the most energetic and positive crewmember on the plane. She breezed down the aisles with the meal service, probably a little too happy judging by the scared faces of some of the passengers as she smiled inanely at them; it *was* the middle of the night after all.

'Breaks are written down on the side,' the purser, Simon, said as they came in with the carts from the duty-free service. 'Sorry it's not a lot,' he apologised.

They all gathered around the paper, the sick bag that had been used to write the timings of the breaks on. Susan was surprised that he had found any left to use.

'Oh, they're split in three,' Gemma remarked flatly, but the undertone of 'what-the-hell' wasn't lost on the others. It was a night flight, everyone was asleep. They all understood that you couldn't have half the crew in bed on a busy day flight, but *everyone* split it in two on a night flight!

Except Martha.

They all looked at Simon, who rolled his eyes. He was professional enough not to say his true feelings, but it was clear he was on the same page as the rest of them. Susan felt her good mood wane slightly. People like Martha really pissed her off, awkward for the sake of being awkward, because they were in the position where no one took them to task. Well it was what it was, an hour would have to do.

'Who wants what break?' Claire asked, taking control and bringing everyone back in the moment. She was poised with her pen ready to assign names to the paltry time slots.

'I'm easy,' Gemma said. 'I don't have far to drive the other end.'

'Can I have last please, I've got to get to Nottingham,' groaned James.

'I don't mind first or second,' added Susan. She just hated last, having to come back and get straight into the breakfast service was nauseating enough on a regular flight.

Claire wrote names next to the break times and they leant in around her, each happy with their assignments, despite their shortness in length. Susan was on first, so she put her cart away quickly and grabbed her bottle of water.

'Okay, I'm off,' she said; a power nap would be the final piece in her recovery. She walked quickly down the aisle to the magic door at the back, her imaginary blinkers firmly on and making eye contact with no one, in case they asked her for something!


The three girls busied themselves getting things ready for breakfast, their breaks over and London getting closer.

'When's everyone flying next?' asked Claire over her shoulder as she filled the coffee pots up.

'Next year,' Susan said smugly. She was excited to get

236

back, this really was her last flight of 2017, and Christmas was going to begin the moment that she got home, beginning with Jeff's party in a couple of days.

'Lucky!' said Claire, who was still full time. 'I've got an Abuja in two days.'

'Oh you poor thing.' Susan did remember the days of being full time, without the flexibility to swap your flights around, and when you barely unpacked your case before you were packing it again.

'New York,' added Gemma, rather enthusiastically.

'Of course,' Claire said, as if she expected no less. 'Where else would you be going!'

Susan felt like she was missing out on something, and that they were both in on it.

'What's in New York?' she asked.

'Her hot date,' teased Claire. Gemma blushed, smiling shyly.

'Oh, lucky you!' Susan said, seeing that whoever it was clearly made Gemma very happy. 'Where did you meet him?'

'Just on a trip,' Gemma said, obviously not ready to divulge all the details to someone she didn't know very well. Claire, however, was always happy to share people's secrets.

'Literally, she didn't even have to leave the hotel,' she laughed.

'Claire!' Gemma exclaimed, wide-eyed. 'I told you in confidence! Sorry, Susan, I didn't really want everyone to know.'

'Oh no worries, hon, I understand.' She understood completely, glad that she hadn't told Claire any of her own secrets.

'It's just that,' she began, clearly not wanting to make Susan feel left out now that things had gone this far, 'it's the hotel manager.'

'Oh!' Susan didn't turn around, couldn't trust her face. 'Wow, okay, I understand why you're keeping that to yourself!'

'You know,' Claire was incorrigible, not fazed by Gemma's reluctance to divulge everything, 'Tony, the *really* hot one!'

'Oh, yes, I know Tony,' Susan said as flatly as she could, her pulse racing. It had been Gemma she had seen him with that night, she realised. Now that she could put a face on the girl in the shadows it was definitely Gemma; same hair, same height, same gorgeous figure. Susan's thoughts were all over the place and she was relieved when the others came back from break moments later, bringing an end to the conversation, Susan would have to think about this another time, in a different frame of mind.

# Chapter 55

Oh, how Susan Harrison's world was changing. The drive home from the flight was spent in reflection, processing thoughts and memories, trying to form a picture of how things stood at this moment in time.

Mark, over.

Luke, over.

Tony, over?

Was Tony over? Could she be as excited to see him now that she knew about Gemma? When the 'others' were faceless, nameless, they didn't exist. But now she was real, *and* she was crew. Susan tried to work out what exactly it was that bothered her about it being crew so much. She had never expected Tony to be monogamous, but now she felt cheapened, like everyone knew she was just another of his many, not anything special. She remembered now how his friend had looked at her when she left the hotel that last time, and now that look seemed to be mocking her. Gemma probably wasn't even the only other crewmember that Tony 'visited'.

If she was honest, the fact that Gemma was ten years

younger than her was a problem too. As much as she was confident in her looks, if she was Tony she would probably prefer Gemma, and that thought was crushing. She glanced in the rear-view mirror at her reflection. The night flight had taken its toll and her eyes looked tired. A few years ago she had prided herself on how fresh she looked at the end of a flight, but things were starting to change. It wouldn't be many more months before she would reach her thirty-sixth birthday, and the thought made her shudder.

She thought about Mario for a moment, her only remaining lover, but he too would probably settle down soon. Perhaps, she thought in a moment of inspiration, she could find some more interests? She hadn't met anyone for a long, long, time, having enough to keep her busy, but she could always start looking.

Susan sank back into her seat, the thought of actively looking for someone to have an affair with not sitting well with her. The others had all happened naturally, no effort required on her part. But now she was that much older, that little bit less confident in herself. Before, she had truly believed that she was irresistible, and she realised now how arrogant that had been. Now she questioned whether she was anything special at all, or if Tony had only been with her because she was easy. She didn't like this last thought, shaking herself off, deciding not to give it any energy. She wasn't completely stupid, and they had all, definitely, been under her spell.

Her phone pinged, and a message from Jeff flashed up on her screen. She smiled, his name bringing her back to reality, the one here and now. She was lucky, Jeff would always adore her, and while Susan Harrison needed all of the others, Susan Kennedy didn't. She was beginning to wonder if perhaps Susan Harrison's days were numbered.

Susan smiled as she listened to Jeff singing away in the shower. She laid out the outfit she had chosen for him on the bed next to hers, taking a moment to appreciate how they complemented each other with the different shades of blue, albeit hers being much more sparkly and Christmassy. Hair and makeup done earlier at the salon, nails on all limbs manicured, she slipped the sequinned dress over her freshly spray-tanned body, and admired the finished look from each angle in the mirror.

'Wow!' Jeff stood in the bathroom door with a huge grin of appreciation on his face.

'Do you like?' Susan stood on her tiptoes, simulating the killer heels she was yet to put on, and doing a twirl.

'Very much,' nodded Jeff. 'You look absolutely stunning.'

Jeff had no idea about her faltering confidence, but she loved him so much right in that moment for saying exactly what she needed him to say.

'Thank you,' she said graciously.

Susan walked over to her dresser and opened the drawer that held all of her occasion jewellery, the expensive pieces that only came out once in a blue moon. To be honest, she preferred the more fashionable dress jewellery that she wore regularly, but tonight she would don diamonds because they were what Jeff had bought her.

'That's odd,' she said as she brushed aside boxes, unable to find what she was looking for.

'What's up?' Jeff asked as he wriggled into his trousers.

'Oh, nothing,' she said, distracted. 'I just can't find some earrings.'

She could have sworn her diamond solitaire earrings were on the top in their little green box the last time that she saw them, but they were nowhere to be seen now. She opened a few other drawers just in case she had misplaced them, but she knew deep down that she hadn't put them anywhere else. They were always in the drawer, and now they were gone.

'Sophia, have you borrowed some diamond earrings from my drawer?' Susan asked casually, trying not to be accusing, standing at her daughter's bedroom doorway.

Sophia shook her head, looking up confused from where she was lying on her bed, reading.

'Okay, no worries, I just can't find them. You haven't seen a little green jewellery box?'

'No.' Again her daughter shook her head.

'That's odd.' Susan shook her own head as she walked back to her room.

'Did she have them?' Jeff was sitting on the side of the bed putting on his shoes.

'No.' Susan wasn't sure what to think of it all. She believed her daughter, like she did about the makeup, but she was the only one who it made sense to suspect.

'I'm sure they'll show up,' Jeff said reassuringly.

'Yes, you're right, maybe I took them away and they're in a bag somewhere.' She knew that she hadn't but it was a feasible explanation. 'Anyway, we had better get going,' she said, looking at her watch.

'I'm ready.' Jeff stood up.

'Very smart.' Susan was impressed with how well he had scrubbed up. 'Go on down, I'll be two minutes.' She just needed to find some alternative jewellery first.

# Chapter 56

The driver dropped them at the end of the street and Susan held Jeff's arm as they walked along to the restaurant in St Katharine's Dock. London was her favourite place to go out, and now in its Christmas finery it looked even more wonderful than usual. It was true that she had been to cities that were taller, more modern, busier, but London just had that perfect balance between the romance of its history and the success of a world leader. She must make more of an effort to come into town, she made a mental note to herself.

They walked towards the restaurant, a wooden three-storey building that had obviously stood there watching over the docks for hundreds of years. Her romantic side pictured people from bygone ages walking these same steps, and she could almost hear their voices. This was the first time she had been to this part of the capital, and she squeezed Jeff's arm to signal her approval. He didn't seem to notice, eyes firmly focussed on the restaurant; obviously he had been here before and the ambience was lost on him somewhat.

Ever the gentleman, Jeff held the door open and Susan walked into the hustle and bustle of the busy venue. Log fires were burning in the far corners, and a sea of people stretched across the huge room, the echoes of a thousand conversations hanging in the air.

'Upstairs.' Jeff must have seen her hesitate, forgotten for a moment that she hadn't been here before. He pointed across the room to the staircase, taking her hand and guiding her through the throng of people. When they reached the first step Susan stopped for a moment to remove her dress coat; she was warmed up now, and ready to make an entrance. She wondered what this feeling was in her stomach, refusing to believe that it was nerves. She had never been nervous before, even when she was meeting a whole group of people she didn't know. She took a deep breath, blocking the thoughts that had plagued her confidence lately. She would be absolutely fine, and they were all going to love her, she told herself. All except Janice!

Jeff led her across the quieter first floor to a long table at the back. She almost didn't recognise Janice at the far end of the table, not because she looked markedly different to the last time she saw her, but because she didn't think she had ever seen her laughing before and that was just what she was doing.

She was relieved to see a familiar round face at the end of the table closest to her, although she couldn't remember his name, but he had worked for Jeff for a long time. She hoped that the pretty girl with the cute brunette bob sitting next to him was his partner, as she could tell immediately that they would get along. Susan hung her jacket on the back of one of the empty seats next to them in the hope that they could sit there. She smiled at the girl, who returned it immediately. Yes, here would be perfect, especially since they were at the opposite end to Janice, who had just adopted her jaded face again as soon as she had seen her. Susan wasn't imagining it, she *really* did hate her.

'Aren't you going to introduce me to everyone?' Susan whispered in Jeff's ear as he hung his jacket on the back of the empty seat next to her, much to her relief. He had been busy acknowledging everyone else, but seemed to have forgotten that she was there.

'I'm sorry, my love,' he apologised. 'You know Nigel and this is his partner Mel.'

'Yes of course.' That was his name, Nigel. 'Good to see you again, and nice to meet you.' She held out her hand and kissed Mel on the cheek. 'It's been so long since I've seen anyone from Jeff's office.'

'Nice to meet you too,' said Mel. 'I don't know anyone here!'

'Oh, well a couple of glasses of wine and I'm sure we will feel like we've been friends for years!' joked Susan, reminded that she, as Jeff's wife, had absolutely no reason to be nervous. She pulled her shoulders back and walked confidently around the table. There were some familiar faces that she was pleased to see, albeit a couple of years older, along with plenty of new ones, and she stopped to talk to each of them. At some point a glass of bubbles was placed in her hand, and just a couple of sips was enough to soften the blow as she reached Janice.

'Janice, how lovely to see you.' People were watching, and there was no way she would let them think that the obvious frostiness was coming from her. She leant down and air kissed her cold cheek, feeling the stiffness, as if kissing a corpse.

'Hello, Susan.' Janice wasn't even trying to hide her dislike. The laughter had gone and she didn't even manage a smile.

'How are you, Janice?' Susan could handle this, she had had more difficult passengers. 'You look absolutely wonderful.'

'Thank you,' she said reluctantly. The people sitting around were all watching, and Susan was sure that they couldn't have failed to notice Janice's behaviour. 'Please excuse me, I have to use the ladies' room.'

Susan stood back, not letting her smile drop as Janice leant down and picked up her bag, pushing back her seat to stand up. She didn't even make eye contact as she stepped past her.

'Hi, I'm Susan,' Susan said cheerfully. If Janice wanted be like that she would make sure she annoyed the hell out of her with her friendliness and popularity. She held out her hand to shake that of the young lad who had been sitting next to her, relieved that he smiled back at her. At least Janice didn't seem to have enlisted anyone else in her hate campaign.

# Chapter 57

She had been right about Mel, they had hit it off immediately. The wine was flowing, in fact her glass never seemed to be empty, and the food came and went, hardly noticed, she was enjoying the conversation so much.

'So, what do you do, Mel?' Susan asked, realising that she had just talked about *her* job for at least the past twenty minutes. Not that Mel had shown any signs of boredom, people generally liked to hear about it, but it was rude nonetheless.

'Oh, I'm really boring, I'm afraid,' she said apologetically. 'I work from home doing accounts and bookkeeping.'

Susan was surprised that this obviously fun and outgoing person had such a, by her own admittance, boring job.

'Oh wow, how did you get into that? You must be very clever!' she said, there was no way she would let her know that she agreed with her description of boring. Ultimately, she was actually more successful in her career than Susan, probably earned more money, so she certainly wasn't going to look down on her for her career choice.

'Yeah,' said Mel, rolling her eyes. 'Unfortunately, I was

clever at school, and my dad was an accountant, so it just happened. I bloody hate it though, I'd much rather do what you do.'

Susan had heard that so many times before. She was lucky though, that she didn't need to earn a fortune, as a part time cabin crew wage wouldn't have kept them in any kind of luxury. She was pretty sure that Nigel must be earning a good wage after all this time with Jeff though, so perhaps Mel wasn't financially tied, she wondered.

'Well we are always recruiting, and you'd be great at it, maybe you should give it a go?' Susan said, meaning it.

'Really? Don't I need languages? Aren't I too old? I'm in my thirties!' Mel was wide-eyed now.

'No,' Susan laughed kindly at the common misconceptions. The days of having to retire from flying in your thirties, or needing to be fluent in other languages were long gone, along with the lucrative contracts. 'Honestly, you'd be great. Have a think about it and if you're still interested when the wine's worn off, come round and see me. I'll help you with the application!'

On cue the waiter filled their glasses and they raised them in a toast. Susan could see Mel's excitement bubbling behind her eyes and she hoped she would hear from her. Suddenly though, her face changed to a more serious one, and she was now looking past Susan. She wondered what she was going to say as she leant in towards her.

'Who is that woman at the other end of the table, and what the fuck is her problem?'

Susan didn't even need to turn around to know that only Janice could have reduced Mel to her first public use of the F word. Not that Susan was averse to it, but it was normally held back until friendships were cemented, *or* she was with crew. She turned around anyway, wanting Janice to feel the looks she had obviously been throwing returned by two pairs of eyes. Her nemesis looked quickly away.

'Oh, that's Janice, or I like to call her Jaded Janice, and for some reason she hates me,' Susan said matter-of-factly, before smiling as she took a sip of her drink.

'You don't say!' Mel was still staring back at her. 'If looks could kill you'd be dead a thousand times over. What's her issue?'

'I have absolutely no idea, but thank you for confirming what I already knew, that she hates me,' Susan said again, shrugging her shoulders nonchalantly, before laughing. She had found the funny side now that she had someone to laugh at it with, glad that she wasn't alone with her suspicions.

'Haven't you said anything to her?' Mel asked.

'No.' Susan wondered for a moment why she had never said anything all those times she had been abrupt to her on the phone, realising that it was probably because she had never got the chance, the dial tone always replacing any opportunity to speak. Even now, when she knew she wasn't imagining things, she would never dream of making a scene, and she hated confrontation anyway.

'Well you're better than me, I would have had it out with her. Does she work with these guys?'

'Yes, she's Jeff's PA.' As she said the words she could see her own thoughts reflected in Mel's eyes. Was Janice jealous of her? Did she have her sights set on her husband? The conversation with Claire jumped out of her memory box, her warning about watching your husband's secretaries.

'Oh,' Mel said, looking down at her glass, obviously unsure of what else to say for a moment. 'Well, don't let her get away with being rude to you, you're the boss's wife! Anyway, let me have your number, I would love to take you up on your offer of help with an application.' She smiled broadly, lightening the situation, and Susan was relieved to change the subject.

Despite trying to ignore it, Susan just couldn't help but notice the daggers that Janice would throw her way every once in a while. It was probably the effects of the wine, but as the evening passed her usual composure was being threatened.

'Long time no see,' she quipped when Jeff finally returned to his seat.

'Sorry, I've been trying to make sure I speak to everyone,' he apologised.

'The pressures of being the boss,' Susan said with as much sympathy as she could muster. She had never been needy and demanding of his attention, in fact she knew that she was always extremely reasonable and understanding, but some things were just too much.

'Honey, please don't think I am being difficult,' she began, speaking quietly so that Jeff had to lean in to hear her. 'I thought it was just me, but other people have noticed it too. Janice keeps on looking at me in a horrible way, and completely blanked me when I spoke to her earlier. Do you have any idea why she seems to be so upset with me?'

Jeff shook his head but said nothing.

'Any chance you could have a word with her as it's

making me feel really uncomfortable?' she asked, trying to sound as mature as she could despite her childish complaints.

'Of course,' Jeff said. She was so relieved that he had taken her seriously. 'I'm sure she hasn't meant to, she's just a bit uncomfortable with women in general.'

'Oh, okay,' said Susan. She supposed, reluctantly, that it could be feasible; she had in fact been surrounded by men when she had been laughing earlier, and Susan couldn't actually recall ever having seen her speak to another woman, but it still didn't make her rudeness okay. 'Here's your chance.'

Janice had just stood up, and Susan nudged Jeff, gesturing in her direction.

'What, now?' Jeff asked, looking at her imploringly.

'No time like the present.' Susan was not letting this opportunity slip. She was afraid that if Jeff didn't sort this out then she may have to say something herself, and she wasn't sure how that would go after so much wine.

Jeff pushed back his seat and stood up reluctantly. Janice was passing with a wide berth, and he excused himself through a few people to head her off. Susan watched him get her attention by touching her arm, and wondered what the enigmatic look that she gave him meant, if it meant anything at all. She turned back around quickly as they both looked in her direction, trusting her husband to deal with things.

A few minutes later the chair next to her moved, signalling Jeff's return. He looked a bit drained, she thought, like he really hadn't enjoyed the *chat* that he had just had. He picked up his glass and took a long drink.

'Everything okay?' Susan asked tentatively, when he

wasn't offering anything up. She felt like an immature teen that had just got her boyfriend involved in a petty row and she felt bad now, she knew that Jeff hated confrontation.

'Yes, fine.' He smiled tightly, his voice controlled. 'She's says she hasn't been off with you, but she's not feeling well so she's going home anyway. You don't have to worry any more about it.'

'Oh.' Susan knew that she hadn't been imagining it, but she could tell that Jeff wasn't going to discuss it anymore. She looked behind her to see Janice heading towards the top of the stairs, and thought for a minute that she looked upset, quickly brushing off the idea and any sympathy that came with it. Her head was hung so that her hair fell forward, and she walked quickly, practically pushing people out of her way. As she held the rail to go down the steps her bag caught on the post at the top. Susan couldn't miss the annoyed look on her face as she unhooked it impatiently. Neither could she miss that it was a beautiful leather Mulberry bag, the same one she had been waiting for these past weeks, the same one on the receipt she had found in Jeff's blazer pocket... from Paris.

# Chapter 58

Oh, the rollercoaster she had been on these past few days. She had tried to be reasonable, to put it to the back of her mind, but the whole thing with Janice just wouldn't go away, going around and around in circles.

'I'm not being paranoid, am I?' she had asked Mel repeatedly that night.

'No, not at all, she definitely has a problem,' her new friend had assured her, time and time again.

So why couldn't Jeff see it? Did he really think that his explanation of her just being uncomfortable with women was enough of an excuse?

Up and down she went. Perhaps Janice really *was* that uncomfortable, but why? Had something happened to her? Was she frightened of being read, judged maybe, for something? Was she really like it with all women though? Susan found that very hard to believe.

And the bag…

AAARgh, Susan shook her head, trying to rid herself of the threatening madness. There was no sense in thinking like this. Just because *she* behaved the way that she did, she had never for a moment believed that Jeff would ever be disloyal, she *knew* that he wouldn't be. She had always trusted him, and she always would, she told herself firmly; no good would come of things being any other way. Besides, there could be many explanations for the bag, and Janice's behaviour…

'Darling, they are here,' Jeff called up the stairs.

'Just coming,' Susan called back in her most amiable Susan Kennedy voice, resetting herself.

Back in the present everything was normal again, she thought, looking around. Her room was just as it always was. Her husband was calling her in his usual loving tone. Everything was okay. Well as okay as they could be when his parents had just arrived.

She walked briskly down the stairs, joining the kids, and the dogs in the hall just as Jeff opened the front door. Jeff's dad stood on the other side hidden behind a tower of presents.

'Merry Christmas,' a voice boomed from behind the parcels.

Susan couldn't help but smile at the looks of joy that the presents and the salutation put on the faces of her children. They were all oblivious to her own personal demons, and she resolved in that moment to forget all of the nonsense. Christmas was going to be wonderful, and Jaded Janice was *not* going to ruin it!

'Merry Christmas,' they all replied in unison, stepping forward to help the old man with his beautifully decorated burdens.

It was like a scene from a Christmas movie, Susan observed, looking at the wide grins on George and Margaret's faces, noses red from the cold, all wrapped up in their winter clothes.

'Come on in out of the cold!' Susan said, ushering them in.

'Oh no, my dear, we have more in the car,' George said cheerfully, turning back to the Bentley.

'I'll help you, Dad.' Jeff followed him.

'Merry Christmas, Margaret,' Susan said with genuine affection, leaning forward to kiss her on the cheek once she was over the threshold.

'You too, dear, and you two.' She leant forward and both of the children stepped up dutifully to kiss her. 'Thank you for having us,' she said softly as she stood upright.

'Oh, anytime, you are always welcome.' Susan was somewhat taken aback by Margaret's gratitude, and her overall demeanour. Something was different and it was a good thing. Maybe she had had an epiphany, like everyone had at points in their life, she wondered.

'Right, straight through here, Dad.' Jeff's voice broke the moment, and Susan laughed to see her husband carrying another tower of presents. His parents had always been generous, but in a less understated way. They would usually drop off a small pile of expensive presents a week or so before Christmas, before their cruise, presents that reflected Margaret's tastes more than the recipients'.

'Oh my goodness, you are far too generous.' Susan looked at Margaret, and thought how happy she seemed as she watched the gifts that she had obviously spent a long time buying and wrapping, finally delivered.

'Well since we are here to see the children unwrap them, I got a bit carried away with things.'

Sophia and Lewis were jumping up and down, like

they were small children again, and for a brief moment Susan felt sad that all of their Christmases hadn't started like this.

They all followed the men into the lounge, the children helping them to put the presents under the tree, eagerly inspecting each one to find their names.

'Well that has got to be the biggest Christmas tree I've seen in my life,' George remarked, hands on hips, looking at the lit up overgrown shrub.

'It looks marvellous in here, Susan,' said Margaret, looking around.

'Thank you.' Susan was loving this new mother-in-law, she could come more often! 'Here, let me take your coats.'

They both handed her their coats and scarves and she carried them through to the hall, hanging them on the coat stand. Two small cases sat by the door and she carried them quickly up the stairs to the guest room, sitting them next to the ottoman at the foot of the bed. She smiled to herself at the perfection of the evening, full of promise for a wonderful Christmas, and all of the turmoil of the last few days was washed away. What mattered was here and now, not there and then, or the ifs and maybes, and here and now was just perfect.

# Chapter 59

Never in all of their years had Susan known her children to wake up so early on Christmas Day, such was their excitement. She had heard other parents groan at their little ones waking at four or five in the morning, but she and Jeff had always marvelled at how theirs would still sleep in until seven, with them sitting up waiting impatiently for them. She suspected that the sheer volume of gifts under the tree was the catalyst for the 5.30 thunder of footsteps, and the excited voices coming from their rooms as they opened their stockings.

'Lewis, bring yours in here,' she heard Sophia whisper loudly, followed by the sound of Lewis dragging his sack across the hall.

'Coming.' She looked at Jeff who was wide awake now too, and they both chuckled at the sound of their offspring trying to be quiet. Susan wrapped her arms around Jeff and hugged his warm body.

'Happy Christmas,' he said, and she looked up to kiss him.

'Happy Christmas, my love,' she replied, eventually

pulling herself up, needing to be privy to whatever was happening along the way.

Tiptoeing in her slippers along the landing she could hear George's snores above the excited whispers of the children. She pushed Sophia's door open slowly and stood silently watching them open their presents. She was sure that neither of them believed in Santa anymore, but despite their questioning she would always refuse to admit that he didn't exist. Anyway, a stocking was a stocking, no matter who delivered it.

The coffee machine gurgled to an end as Susan lifted the turkey and all of its trimmings into the oven. She may have cheated with some of the accompaniments, ordering them already prepared, but the turkey was her centrepiece and she would take all credit for it later when it sat in the middle of the table.

'Merry Christmas.' Margaret walked into the kitchen. Susan hadn't heard her coming above the noise of the coffee machine and the Christmas music that was playing on the radio.

'Oh, merry Christmas, Margaret, you're up and dressed early!'

Her mother-in-law was already dressed in her wool skirt and twin set, pearls draped around her neck. Her hair was set and makeup applied, and all by 7.30.

'Oh, I'm always up early, my dear,' she informed her, and Susan wondered if she probably should have known this fact. 'Can I help?'

'No, no,' Susan dismissed. 'Everything is under control here. Would you like a coffee?'

'That would be lovely.'

Susan poured two cups of coffee, aware that she herself was still in her dressing gown and without makeup.

'There you go.' She placed the porcelain mug down on the island. 'Please forgive me a moment, I'm just going to go and pop some clothes on before I get breakfast ready. The children are in the lounge with their presents from Santa.'

'Of course,' Margaret conceded, needing no persuasion to go and find her grandchildren.

'Has something happened to your mother?' Susan asked as she applied her makeup.

'What do you mean?' Jeff asked, from the ensuite.

'Oh, it's a good thing,' Susan said quickly, suspecting that Jeff was expecting a complaint. 'I've just never seen her so.... nice.'

Jeff appeared in the mirror, smiling.

'I know what you mean.' Susan was happy to have his agreement. 'I think she's just realised what she's been missing out on all these years. She's been phoning me this past month about what the children like, and I think the Christmas spirit has just got to her.'

Susan nodded, the explanation seeming feasible.

'A bit like Scrooge,' Jeff joked and Susan laughed at the comparison.

'Well whatever it is, I like it,' she said.

'Me too,' Jeff agreed. 'Right, I'm going down.'

'Won't be long.'

Susan was nearly ready, and she knew the perfect thing to finish off her outfit. She dug deep in amongst the boxes in her jewellery drawer. Many years ago, Margaret had given her a ring, an heirloom, a sapphire surrounded by diamonds. It was very beautiful, but at the time her dislike of the woman, which she believed to be mutual, had made it very ugly in her eyes. Now though, she would wear it happily, and she hoped that Margaret would approve.

Ten minutes later, with the entire contents of the drawer out, Susan sighed in frustration; it was nowhere to be found. Nor had her earrings reappeared. She couldn't help but presume there was a connection, although she hadn't seen the ring for years, so it could have been missing for a long time. She made a mental list of what she thought had been in the drawer, and nothing else seemed to be gone, so she was pretty sure that they hadn't been burgled. So where had they gone?

Well, today was not the day for a full inquiry, for questioning Sophia, or worrying anyone, but she would have to come back to it, she thought as she put everything back. She was disappointed that she couldn't wear the ring, sad that her opportunity to please Margaret was gone, and infuriated that someone had just taken it. She filed the thought for later.

# Chapter 60

The dining room had been strictly off limits this past week as Susan had laid the table and added touches to it daily. They seldom used the room anyway, so it had been her studio for creating her work of art without affecting their routines. She lit the candles on the two candelabra that sat at either end and stood back to admire the white and silver decor. Napkins in sparking rings sat on diamanté-rimmed charger plates, crystal glasses stood proudly, polished and reflecting the flames that now flickered. The ivy and foliage that stretched along the centre screamed Christmas, and the silver crackers that she had ordered from Harrods were laid at each seat, waiting to be pulled and reveal their luxury surprises. She dimmed the lights on the chandelier that hung in the centre of the room, before finally opening the door, ready to share her work with everyone.

'Wow.' Lewis's eyes were wide, first to enter, and he dashed to the table to find his name on a place card.

'Well you've truly excelled yourself this year,' Jeff said, his arm around her, squeezing, as they watched the others take their seats.

'Thank you,' she said, accepting the compliment which she knew she deserved.

'I'll be back in a moment with starters,' she said cheerfully, grateful for the hostess trolley that usually sat in the larder unused. She had even decorated it with left-over Christmas decorations and it was in the kitchen ready to wheel in the many courses that she had prepared, albeit with a little help from M&S!

Happily exhausted, Susan sank into the chesterfield and took the glass of champagne that Jeff offered her. Dinner had been a complete success, and she deserved it more than ever.

'Can we open presents now?' Sophia asked, raising her eyebrows like a puppy to give her the best chance of success.

'Of course, darling,' Susan said; everyone was gathered around now and this was the perfect time to start.

The paper frenzy that followed was like none that she had ever seen before as the children opened one present after another, adding each gift to their individual present mountains. She watched George and Margaret beaming as they received one hug after another, relieved when they finally reached the ones that she had bought them so that she could have some hugs too.

'This is for you.' Sophia put a gift bag on the floor in front of her, standing and waiting for her to open it. She turned the tag over to see who it was from.

*To My Beautiful Wife*
*All My Love*
*Jeff*

Susan looked at Jeff and smiled in anticipation. Everyone was watching her now as she carefully opened the large bag and removed the tissue paper. A small blue box sat on the top, and she took it out slowly. She opened the lid to reveal a beautiful diamond eternity ring which took her breath away for a moment.

'You liked it in Dubai,' Jeff said, almost shyly.

'I did,' Susan nodded reflectively, remembering how they had looked in the jeweller's window on the way back from the restaurant, and also remembering its huge price tag. 'I mean I do, it's beautiful, Jeff, thank you.'

'Let me put it on.' Jeff took the box from her, lifting out the ring and sliding it onto her wedding finger. Everyone had gone silent, the beauty and romance of the moment not even lost on the youngest. Susan kissed Jeff, looking back down at the ring that was sparkling insanely.

'What else is in there?' Lewis was bored with the jewellery now obviously, and was peering into the bag that was far too big to hold just that small box.

'Oh yes,' Susan said, excited to see what else her wonderful husband had bought her.

'Ooh, very nice,' said Margaret as Susan held up the cashmere coat. It was very tasteful, she had to admit, wondering if he had had any help in choosing it. She had known Jeff to enlist the help of a personal shopper before, and suspected that he may have done so this time.

'I'm a very lucky lady,' Susan said humbly.

Slowly the pile of presents was distributed, everyone happy with their caches, and Jeff fighting a losing battle with clearing up the paper. Susan sighed as she stood up, ending the break that she had taken out of martyrdom to help him, unable to look at the mess anymore. As she stuffed the last of the paper into the bag she looked back at the tree that seemed quite sad now, without its offerings. Deep down something was niggling her, and she thought hard about what it was. She felt disappointed for some reason, despite the diamonds on her finger, like she had expected more.

The bag, that was it, she had expected the bag. The one from Paris. The same one as Janice had.

# Chapter 61

Oh, the unwelcomness of this new emotion. Susan paced up and down the bedroom, controlling her breathing. Everyone was downstairs but she had needed to get away for a moment, think this over, deal with this insecurity.

Was Jeff having an affair with Janice?

She looked at the receipt that she held in her hand, that she had kept when she put his jacket in the cleaners that day, in case she needed to return *her* bag. The evidence was there, staring at her, but was it absolutely true, or was there another explanation? Would she be naive to believe anything else?

And if he was having an affair, what did that mean? She looked at her ring, the *eternity* ring that he had put lovingly on her finger just an hour ago. Surely you only give an *eternity* ring to someone you are going to spend an *eternity* with?

She knew that he loved her, yes that wasn't in question, he adored her, and their life together, so he wouldn't leave her for Janice, would he?

She shook her head. No, he wouldn't leave, she felt certain of that, well almost certain.

So, if he was having an affair, what did that mean? She asked herself again. She thought of Susan Harrison, how she was able to have affairs without attachment, without any reflection on what she had here, with Jeff and their family. Maybe he was just doing the same? Maybe that was why Janice hated her, because she knew he would never leave her?

*Maybe,* she thought, trying to get control of her imagination, maybe he wasn't even having an affair? That there was another explanation for the bag, and that Janice just hated her because she was jealous?

Yes, that was it. Susan stood still and nodded, that was a much more likely scenario, and the one she was going to stick with. Suddenly her world that had been swirling around her like a tornado began to fall back into place, things dropping back to where they should be. Jeff was a good man, a far better person than her, and he didn't deserve to be judged by her standards. As she put him back on his pedestal in her mind she felt guilty, really guilty, for the first time ever. Guilty for how she had been, for disrespecting him, for taking him for granted. He deserved so much better.

'Everything okay?' Jeff asked as she walked back into the kitchen. He looked a little concerned, perhaps she hadn't hidden her distress as well as she thought when she had excused herself.

'Yes, of course,' Susan smiled, heading for the champagne fridge. 'Everything is perfect.'

She would ask him about the bag one day, when she could say it without emotion, and she knew he would give her a sensible explanation. But not today, not at

Christmas. All that mattered was here and now, she told herself; it was becoming her mantra.

# Chapter 62

Susan loved the whole month that ran up to Christmas, but now that it was over, and the New Year loomed, everything had lost its shine. The tree was starting to look tired, and the decorations seemed pointless now that the big day had gone. She reflected on the success of it, the picture-perfect family Christmas, trying to eliminate all thoughts of Janice and the bag from her memory, but they just wouldn't disappear completely. After five days she could take no more when Jeff asked her for the hundredth time if she was okay, as she clearly was not as good at hiding some emotions as she was others.

'I know there's something wrong, please tell me what it is so I can do something about it,' he implored as she took her makeup off.

'It's just something really stupid, you'll think I've gone mad,' she said nervously, aware that she would have to say it out loud now, keeping her back turned from him.

'Oh, for God's sake just say it.' Jeff sounded frustrated, and she needed him to be relaxed in order to take what she was going to say the way she hoped that he would.

'Okay, okay, sorry,' she apologised, opening her drawer and taking out the receipt. She stood up and walked over to where he lay in bed.

'What's this?' He was clearly confused, taking the receipt and trying to translate it.

'It's a receipt, Jeff,' Susan said as calmly as she could. 'For a Mulberry handbag, one that I actually really wanted myself.'

Jeff was still looking at the receipt, saying nothing. She was obviously going to need to explain further if he was to say what she needed him to say.

'I found it in your blazer when I had it cleaned for Dubai, and I kept it because I presumed you had bought it as a gift for me.'

'Oh,' Jeff said slowly, the penny dropping. He still didn't look up, nor did he say anything else.

'I noticed that Janice had that exact bag at the Christmas dinner.'

There, it was out, everything was said that needed to be said, and she held her breath as she waited for her suspicions to be proved wrong.

'And you thought what?' Jeff was looking at her with an expression she was unfamiliar with. Was it disdain, annoyance? Was he offended?

'I thought that maybe you had bought it for Janice,' Susan said, thinking it best not to add that she had thought they were having an affair.

'I did,' Jeff said flatly, and Susan's stomach felt as if he had just punched her in it. He was looking straight at her, and seemed to be daring her to question him as to why he would have bought Janice the bag.

'Oh.' Susan looked at the floor and bit her lip, thinking

that she might cry.

'I bought it for her because she lost her purse, and had no money, and she paid me back,' he said deliberately.

Susan melted with relief, looking up sheepishly to meet his stare.

'Sorry,' she apologised again. 'I told you you'd think I'd gone mad.'

'Come here, you madwoman.' Jeff's smile was a welcome change from the other look he had held throughout, and she jumped into his arms before he had a chance to change it again. She stopped herself from defending her suspicions, because that would have meant bringing up Janice's behaviour towards her again, and that, she knew, never went well. He had explained the bag, and she believed him, that was enough.

*How about that coffee next week?* Susan texted Mel the next morning. She had found an ally in Mel that night at the meal, and now that she needed someone to talk to she was glad that they had swapped numbers. Susan Kennedy's life had always been so predictable before that she had never needed close friends. The girls from the gym were usually enough to tide her over with female conversation between flights, but with all of the emotional ups and downs of the last few days she really felt that she needed somebody who would listen, and someone who wouldn't think she was imagining things.

*Sounds great, when and where?* Mel's message came back almost immediately.

*Come here, I'll make us brunch and we can talk about*

*your application!* (*And then we can talk about Janice*), she added silently.

*What day, and what's your address?*

*Monday if that's good for you?* Susan added her address.

*Perfect*

Monday couldn't come soon enough. There was just the matter of a meal out for New Year in between, and getting these decorations down, she mused, feeling a little overwhelmed by the scale of *that* operation. The sound of someone coming in the back door startled her for a moment, until she realised that it was Lucy, and her spirits lifted. Christmas had been amazing but it had been a lot of work, and she had missed her helper immensely.

'Lucy, I'm so happy to see you!' She wondered if Lucy appreciated just how indispensable she was.

'Thank you.' Lucy looked amused, and Susan suspected that she did realise.

'How was your Christmas?' she asked carefully.

'Oh, it was lovely actually, quiet but lovely.'

Susan couldn't help but notice how relaxed Lucy looked, as if her troubles had lifted and she had enjoyed her break. Like the superstar that she was though, within seconds she had cleared the kitchen sides and normality was being restored. Susan watched her with overwhelming affection, thinking that she really must talk to Jeff about giving her a pay rise, it was the season of goodwill after all!

# Chapter 63

'Welcome,' Susan beamed as her soon-to-be new best friend got out of her car. She had decided that now Susan Harrison wasn't so busy, Susan Kennedy needed more of a social life, and that was going to start with Mel.

'Hi,' Mel waved at her, but she seemed a little confused, looking around her before heading over to the house.

'Come on in,' Susan beckoned. She was used to people being overwhelmed when they first came here. Some would gush about how beautiful it all was, but those like Mel would just be a bit uneasy for a while, until she settled in. It was okay, she would have her relaxed in no time.

Mel was still verging on mute when she led her into the kitchen and poured her a Buck's Fizz; it was brunch after all, and brunch always went along with fizz.

'Happy New Year,' toasted Susan, prompting Mel to pick up her glass. Maybe a few bubbles would relax her and bring back the Mel from the party, she hoped.

'Happy New Year,' said Mel picking up her glass, still looking around, still distracted.

'I'm so glad you could come over,' smiled Susan. She

wondered if she needed to tone down the enthusiasm, if she was being overbearing. 'Please, take a seat.' She led the way over to the table, pulling out a chair for herself. Mel followed her and sat opposite. She was smiling, that was a good thing, but it still seemed a bit forced. This wasn't going how she had hoped it would, and she was unsure how to handle it.

'Lovely house,' said Mel eventually.

'Thank you.' Susan was well used to the compliment. 'Are you hungry? I made us some food.'

She stood up again to get the platters that she had carefully prepared, bringing them over and setting them down on the table. Fresh fruits and pastries, along with meats and salmon, Susan had worked hard that morning to recreate some of the many brunches she had enjoyed around the world.

'Wow, you really shouldn't have gone to so much trouble, this looks amazing.'

'It's nothing really, I love entertaining,' Susan said, not wanting her to feel any more overwhelmed than she obviously was. 'Oh, clumsy me.' Susan wiped a piece of the cream cheese from her green dress.

'So, have you got that application in yet?' Susan asked, handing Mel a plate.

'Not yet, Christmas has been busy,' she replied. 'But I will do, very soon.'

'Well let me know when you do, I have a friend who does a bit in recruitment that might be able to help you out.'

'That's brilliant, thank you.'

Ah, that was better, thought Susan, now she seemed to have her attention. Another ten minutes or so talking about her and she could move the conversation on to Janice.

'Honestly, you'd be brilliant,' Susan gushed. 'And you could still do some of your bookkeeping around it, if you wanted to?'

'Hmmm, only if I *really* need the money. I'd rather not taint my new glamorous lifestyle with people's boring accounts.' Mel rolled her eyes, leaning over to select some salmon and a fresh bagel from the platter.

'I hear you,' Susan agreed. 'So how was your Christmas?'

Lucy walked into the room with her gloves on and various cleaning products in her hand, placing them down on the kitchen side. She was such a constant in the house that Susan hardly noticed her there, only turning to see her when she noticed Mel staring at her.

'Mel?' Her guest was absolutely transfixed on her housekeeper, not even chewing the food in her mouth as she watched her. Lucy on the other hand was oblivious, standing with her back to them, getting on with her work diligently, busying herself in the background like she usually did. Mel turned back to look at her, looking even more confused now than when she had first arrived, eyes wide but not focused on her, like she was a million miles away thinking about something monumental.

Now Susan was confused too; surely Mel had seen a cleaner before? Surely Jeff didn't pay Nigel so little that her life was so far removed from this? She knew she had more than most, but it wasn't Buckingham Palace, and Mel's behaviour was beginning to be a little odd.

'Mel?' Susan prompted again. 'Is everything okay?'

Mel shook her head, not in a 'no' way, more in a bringing herself back into the moment way.

'I'm sorry, I was just thinking about something.' She put her bagel, which she had barely touched, back onto her plate and dusted off her hands, looking back at Lucy again.

'Who's that?' she asked, whispering, leaning forward, like she didn't want her to hear.

'Oh,' Susan said, so obviously it was the presence of a cleaner that had made Mel so uncomfortable, perhaps she really was living in a very different world. 'That's Lucy, my housekeeper.'

Hearing her name Lucy turned around for just a second.

'I don't know what I'd do without her,' Susan smiled at her. She turned back to Mel who now looked as if she had seen a ghost, and for a moment she wondered if she had choked on her food, such was the paleness of her face.

*Crash!*

Lucy dropped something on the floor, distracting her from asking Mel if she was okay, again. Without even stopping to pick whatever it was up, Lucy shot out of the back door, gone in the blink of an eye.

Susan sat speechless for a moment, both at Lucy's skittish behaviour and at Mel's. She was starting to think that it had perhaps been the wine that had blurred her judgement that night, and that this person was possibly not 'friend' material at all. She was verging on being quite odd, if Susan was honest with herself.

And what was with Lucy? She had seemed so normal this morning, and now *she* was acting weird again! Susan took a big sip of her Buck's Fizz, suddenly feeling like the only sane one in the house.

'Have you finished?' Susan asked cordially after another minute of silence, not waiting for an answer before picking up the food that had hardly been touched. She couldn't sit here much longer making conversation with someone who looked like a rabbit caught in the headlights. As for changing the subject to Janice, that would be just too much effort. No, brunch was over, she decided, her life was too short to spend it like this.

'Susan.' Mel's voice surprised Susan as she put the food down on the side. She sounded serious, and when she turned to look at her she could see that she was back in the moment, the weird confused look replaced by one of concern. 'You might want to sit down.'

# Chapter 64

Susan couldn't believe what Mel was telling her. No wonder she had been acting weird, she would have been exactly the same if she had been her. She had been in this house before, only it wasn't her house, it was Lucy's, and she had been here with Lucy's 'friends'.

'Are you absolutely sure?' she asked again, knowing the answer but not wanting to believe it. She couldn't work out how Lucy had ended up inviting 'friends', and people that she obviously didn't know, to *her* home, and pretending it was hers. It was all just too bizarre.

'Oh, Susan, I wish I wasn't, but I don't think there is an exact copy of this house anywhere around here, with Lucy's identical twin in it.'

Susan nodded; no, that would be a bad TV show.

'Oh, and I'm ninety-nine per cent sure that she was wearing that dress you have on.'

Susan looked down at her dress and had a sudden urge to tear it off. She felt violated somehow. Lucy had not only been playing lady of the manor, but she had been wearing her clothes as well. What else had she done?

All manner of thoughts started to go through her mind. Had she worn her underwear? Been through her things? Worn her jewellery?

Susan must have gasped out loud when she thought of the jewellery, because Mel leant forward and laid her hand over the top of her clenched fist.

'What the hell do I do now?' Susan looked at Mel, who had now become the rational and focussed one in the room.

'I guess you need to talk to her, when you have had some time to think about it.'

Susan nodded. Yes, she needed to calm down first, rationalise it all, perhaps it wasn't as bad as it seemed. Would she really have taken the jewellery though? Surely Lucy wouldn't have done that? But she didn't know Lucy as well as she thought she did, did she?

'I should probably let you get on, I'm sure you'll need a bit of quiet time to decide what you're going to do.' Mel was standing up, looking down at her bleakly. 'Don't get up, I can see myself out.'

Susan looked up and nodded.

'Call me if you need me.'

'Thanks, Mel, and I'm sorry you got dragged into all of this.' Susan was fighting a mix of emotions, from anger that her perfect life had been hijacked, to feeling vulnerable.

'Oh don't worry, I just hope you sort it out, I'm sure she never meant any harm.'

Susan nodded again; if this practical stranger could extend sympathy to the perpetrator, then surely she could? Yes, that would be how she would approach it, sympathetically, she would hear her out.

* * *

Lucy sat in her armchair and rocked back and forth. She knew the woman had recognised her, she could see it, and she knew that she would tell Mrs Kennedy. So that was it, her moment of madness had cost her a job that she loved, and here she was with a pile of bills to pay and no way to pay them. Why, oh why had she been so stupid as to worry about what Kate and Natasha thought of her? They didn't matter, and yet she had been so reckless because of them.

When there was a knock on the door she knew who it was, and for a moment she thought she might just pretend to be out. Her boss wasn't stupid though, she would have seen her car out front, and she owed her an explanation, she deserved that at least.

'Come in,' she said morosely, holding the door open. Any other day, under any other circumstances she would have felt ashamed to invite someone like Mrs Kennedy into her humble home, but today she didn't care, it didn't matter. Her boss walked down the hall, her head hanging, without saying a word. It wasn't up to her to do the talking, Lucy knew that she was the only one that needed to do that.

'Please sit down.' She gestured to the worn sofa that was covered in a mink throw. The cat dozed peacefully at one end, not a care in the world, and they both watched him for a moment.

'I'm so sorry.' Lucy finally broke the silence, tears welling up in her eyes.

'But why?' asked Mrs Kennedy, who looked equally upset.

Lucy started from the beginning, leaving nothing out. From the first day when she had bumped into Kate at

M&S to how Natasha had threatened to come around unannounced if she didn't invite them. Mrs Kennedy just sat silently, listening.

'But my clothes, Lucy,' she said finally when she had finished.

'I know, I know.' Lucy shook her head as she held it in her hands. 'I don't have a lot, and I couldn't afford to buy expensive clothes to impress them. I know it was unacceptable.'

Mrs Kennedy was still looking at her, and she couldn't bear to see the hurt look in her eye. She had always been so nice to her, she didn't deserve this.

'I don't know what happened,' Lucy continued. She needed to make this better, for both of them. 'It was all after my mum died. I wasn't sleeping, wasn't thinking straight. I think I'd gone a little bit mad.'

Mrs Kennedy nodded; she seemed to accept the explanation.

'But I promise it is all over now. I've learnt my lesson.' She looked at the pile of letters. 'I got into debt trying to keep up with them, but they weren't even real friends. If they knew I was only a cleaner, living in this flat, they would never have wanted to know me any more than they had done at school.'

Mrs Kennedy was nodding again, still leaning forward with her elbows on her knees. She looked as if she needed Lucy to make it all right, like she couldn't deal with anything less than complete justification, and she hoped that she had given her enough. She had no more to offer, she had just laid out every grubby detail of what had happened, told her absolutely everything.

'So,' she said slowly, looking at the letters. 'Is that why

you took the jewellery?

'Excuse me?' Lucy wondered if she had heard right. What was she asking exactly?

'The jewellery, Lucy.' Mrs Kennedy was looking straight at her.

'What jewellery?' Lucy had absolutely no idea what she was talking about. Yes, she had borrowed makeup and clothes, but accessorising the clothes was far beyond her humble abilities.

'The diamond earrings and the ring that have gone missing, Lucy.'

She didn't like the tone that her guest was using now, it was serious, accusing. Was she suggesting that she had taken jewellery to pay off her debts? Oh no, she may have gone a bit mad but she would NEVER steal anything, EVER.

'I have absolutely no idea what you are talking about!' Lucy said finally, trying to control the indignation in her voice. 'I would never steal anything, from anyone!'

'But Lucy you just told me that you are in debt, those diamonds would easily pay off a credit card bill or two.'

Oh, the nerve of it! Lucy could feel the hairs starting to stand up on the back of her neck. Yes, she had done wrong, and yes, she was sorry, but how *dare* she accuse her of stealing her jewellery!

'I have worked for you for many years.' Lucy was talking slowly now, lips pursed, needing to be taken seriously. 'I have never, and would never steal *anything* from you or anyone else.'

'Nobody else could have taken them, Lucy,' Susan said, looking at her as if she was reasoning with a child. 'It's okay, I understand you weren't yourself, and we can work something out about getting them back.'

'How dare you.' Lucy stood up, putting herself in the powerful position, looking down on this spoilt cow for once. 'How dare you accuse me of stealing your things. I have never been anything but trustworthy and loyal, and I have just told you everything about my moment of madness, but I will not be accused of stealing!'

'But, Lucy,' Mrs Kennedy began.

'No, get out of my home.' She pointed her finger dramatically towards the door. 'I'm no thief! I may not be perfect, but neither are you, and if you want to start throwing accusations around I could throw a few at you.'

Mrs Kennedy was still sitting down, mouth open, speechless throughout the outburst.

'Leave my nephew alone, he has a family now, and doesn't need the likes of you, with all your airs and graces leading him astray.'

There, it was said! Lucy stood firm with her hands on her hips, catching her breath.

'I see,' Mrs Kennedy said softly, standing up.

'I'll be in as usual tomorrow,' Lucy added as her boss walked up the hall.

It was several minutes later that the adrenalin on which Lucy had obviously been running subsided. She had shocked herself at her own confidence. It could have gone so differently had she not accused her of stealing. She probably would have resigned, unable to work there now that her shameful actions had been uncovered. But no, why should she quit, she thought angrily, be without a job, because of the opinions of that stuck-up bitch. She had always thought she liked her, but now it was very clear that she looked down at her, thought of her as scum. Because only scum stole from others. No, she wasn't going anywhere, she wasn't being treated like that by someone who blatantly cheated on her husband, not that he was perfect either.

# Chapter 65

'I bought you something,' Jeff declared as he walked into the kitchen carrying a large paper bag. Susan had been a million miles away, and gasped as she recognised the brand. She took it off him quickly, taking out its beautifully wrapped contents and laying it on the kitchen island. Tearing open the paper, she opened the box underneath, and pulled out the drawstring cloth bag. The smell of leather made her breathe in deeply as she revealed the bag that she had coveted for so long.

'Oh, Jeff, you shouldn't have,' she said, although she didn't really mean it.

'I couldn't bear to see how disappointed you were after Christmas.' He was grinning at her, knowing that he had done well.

Susan put the bag down and flung her arms around Jeff's neck. He had no idea what she had been through today, and he never would. There was no way that she could tell him about Lucy, because if he took it up with her, and he would, she was sure to tell him about Luke. So, she had spent the afternoon in reflection on herself, and now that this wonderful man stood here making possibly the worst day of her life wonderful she knew what she needed to do.

'I love you, Jeff, you are my whole world,' she said, staring into his eyes so that he knew how much she meant it.

'And you are mine, my love,' he grinned back, kissing her softly on the lips.

For all of her indiscretions, Susan had never for a moment thought that this wasn't enough, that everything she had wasn't perfect. No, she had always known that, but she had been stupid, self-absorbed and wrapped up in her own vanity. This man here though, he would love her when she got old, when she didn't look quite as good. He didn't have a nutty ex-wife or kids with someone else, nor was he sleeping with multiple other people. No, he was all hers, and he was enough. She looked over at the envelope on the kitchen side, just as Jeff saw it and picked it up.

'What's this?' he asked, turning it over.

'A passport form,' she said coyly.

'Has yours run out?'

'Nope,' she said, teasing him.

'I'm confused,' he said, though he was smiling, amused by her guessing game antics.

'I thought it was time I changed my name at work,' she said. 'Susan Harrison doesn't exist anymore, I am going to be one hundred per cent Susan Kennedy now, my love.'

'Oh.' He looked pleased, but the significance of it was clearly a little lost on him. He had always just accepted her explanation of it being too complicated to change the names in her passport and visas at the same time, unbothered by her having kept Harrison at work, not realising what that had truly meant. Well Susan Harrison was gone now, she had threatened Susan Kennedy's perfect life and she couldn't risk her causing any more damage.

Susan sat at the kitchen island and admired the new handbag. It could have been a cheap one, the price didn't matter, but the fact that he had seen her disappointment and gone and got it was the loveliest gesture he had ever made. Now it didn't matter about Janice having one, she had bought her own after all!

Susan applied a layer of her best cream, smoothing it into her body. She slipped into the lace negligee that she had never worn for Jeff before. If she was to succeed at being Susan Kennedy one hundred per cent, then she needed to put in the same efforts for her husband as Susan Harrison had done for her beaux. She slipped on her heels that made her legs look six feet long and nodded in approval at herself in the mirror.

'Wow,' said Jeff as she walked provocatively past him, sitting himself up in anticipation.

Susan watched Jeff sleep with a serene smile on her face. Yes, this could work, he could be enough for her. She slipped out of the bed and walked silently to her dresser, sitting down on the stool. The light from the lamp reflected off her long earrings, and she released their clasps, putting them back into their box. Pulling open the drawer she put the small box in, stopping in her tracks as she went to close it. There at the back was a small green box, *the* small green box. She took it out and opened it, confirming what she suspected. Inside were the missing earrings. A few moments later she found the ring too, her hand shaking as she put it back.

They hadn't been there this morning when she had taken the earrings out, she was sure of it. Which meant Lucy had had little or no chance to put them back. She felt nauseous, disgusted at herself for accusing her loyal employee, no wonder she had been so upset!

So then who?

It could only have been Sophia, she realised. She remembered her own curiosity as a child, being drawn to sparkly things like a magpie. Perhaps she was just frightened of getting into trouble, had never meant to keep them so long. She'd probably been showing them off to her friends on Instagram! Yes, that was it, Susan was sure that she had finally reached the right conclusion. She was annoyed of course, that whole ugly scene with Lucy could have been avoided, but when she pictured her daughter's sweet face she couldn't be mad. No, she would let it go, they were back now, and she couldn't face another showdown, whoever it was with.

As she lay in the bed trying to get to sleep Susan felt anxious about the next day. She would have to apologise to Lucy, and she hoped that Lucy would accept her apology considering how much the accusation had obviously upset her. Anyway, it wasn't as if she was completely blameless, it was her own weird behaviour that had started all of this, she reasoned lamely.

Susan reached over to the bedside table and picked up her phone; if she texted Lucy now then it was done, hopefully for good. Laying it back down a minute later she took a moment to take in the true enormity of the problem; that Lucy could ruin her life at the drop of a hat if she was ever so inclined. She felt the weight of the grey cloud that hung over her, but maybe that was karma, something she was going to have to live with for the things that she had done.

# Chapter 66

Jeff lay next to his wife, pretending to be asleep. Everything had gone well, and he hoped that he had dodged the bullet this time. He wondered if he would ever be able to get out of this awful mess that he found himself in. Janice had him over a barrel and she was upping her demands all of the time.

It had just been a moment of madness two years ago, a one-night stand after a boozy office party. Yes, he found her attractive, any man would, but he would never have crossed the line if she hadn't used all of her womanly powers on him. He had been helpless to resist her and, in his defence, Susan was showing him little interest at the time, always mentioning his thickening waistline. Janice had made him feel that she wanted him, that he was a catch.

That should have been the end of it though, he had been wracked with guilt and had told her that it could never happen again. But no, Janice wanted more, and if he couldn't give her more on an emotional level then he would have to buy her silence. Not only was he now paying the rent on her apartment, but she expected gifts too.

He had practically had to beg her for the jewellery back. He was annoyed at his own stupidity, thinking that Susan wouldn't notice a few small things gone, she had so much after all, and he really thought that he was taking things which she never wore. He should have just bought Janice some jewellery, it was a clumsy move.

Then there was Paris, she had insisted on coming, even when he had said that Susan was too, that hadn't even deterred her. The bag, the bag that nearly cost him his marriage, just another of her endless demands. If he protested she always gave him the other option, leave Susan and be with her properly, and for him that was no option at all.

Once, he had tried to call her bluff and told her that it was all finished. She had actually come to his home, played with his children, and shown him that he wasn't getting rid of her that easily, in case he had any doubts. If only he had known that Lucy was in the kitchen when he had argued with her in the hall. She had never said anything, but he knew that she knew, it was in her face whenever she looked at him.

He wracked his brains, trying to find the answer, trying to work out how to end it all. Maybe he should just tell Susan, get it out in the open and hope she forgave him? No, he couldn't risk it, couldn't risk losing her.

A grey cloud had hung over him all of this time, but he had learnt to live with it, the consequence of his actions, the karma that he deserved for what he had done.

# Chapter 67

Lucy walked boldly through the back door the next morning. Mrs Kennedy had messaged her last night and apologised for her false accusations. She had accepted the apology, but she would never forget how she had made her feel. Nevertheless, a pay rise was on the cards, and a job was a job.

'Good morning, Lucy,' said Mr Kennedy in that sickly nice tone he had used on her ever since she had heard him arguing with that tart. She nodded at him, that would do. He grabbed his jacket and left the room, as he always did now when their paths crossed.

'Oh, good morning, Lucy.' Mrs Kennedy walked in, all smiles, as if yesterday had never happened. Lucy nodded at her too; she wasn't ready for small talk or falseness. She cleared the empty bowls from the breakfast table and carried them over to the sink. Looking out of the window she could see the blue skies in the distance, and marvelled at how the weather could be so dramatically different in the same small area. Looking straight up she could see the huge grey cloud that was hanging right over this house, and the irony wasn't lost on her. Despite them not finding out about each other's indiscretions, she was quite sure that the Kennedys would be living under their own grey clouds for a very long time to come. Karma was a bitch.

# Acknowledgements

*When I wrote book one in The Osprey Series, Because She Could, it was just a hobby, something to do in my hotel room on my layovers. It amused my friends, whose characters were exaggerated in it, and my fellow crew who could relate so well to the protagonist and her job as a flight attendant.*

*Never did I foresee that it would be the first book in a series, and that just six months later I would be releasing Under Grey Clouds. For that I thank every single person who sent me a message to say they enjoyed my debut novel, or a photo of them reading it across the world, and for the numerous kind comments that I read over and over every time I doubt myself. My friends, my family, my colleagues; the kind people who read through this one before I finalised it. Also, the amazing people I have discovered along the way who have turned it from my humble manuscript to the book on the shelf that it is now.*

*So here I am now starting book three, and my journey continues, thank you to everyone who has been with me along the way so far. Please keep sending me the messages and the photos!*

*Love always*
*Kaylie xxx*

# And Finally...

If you have enjoyed Under Grey Clouds, I would be eternally grateful if you could take a minute to leave a review, they are so important to us writers!

Like the main characters in The Osprey Series, I want nothing more than for my books to travel, so please send me your photos of you reading them! Check out my Instagram account **@kayliekaywritesbooks** or my Facebook page **Novels by Kaylie Kay** for their journeys so far.

You can stay up to date with future releases in the series and contact me at:

www.kayliekaywrites.com